CATCALL

Also by Linda Newbery

At the Firefly Gate
Lost Boy

CATCALL

LINDA NEWBERY

Illustrated by
Ian P. Benfold Haywood

First published in Great Britain in 2006
by Orion Children's Books
a division of the Orion Publishing Group Ltd
Orion House
5 Upper St Martin's Lane
London WC2H 9EA

A catalogue record for this book is
available from the British Library.

ISBN-13: 978 1 84255 125 7
ISBN-10: 1 84255 125 6

Printed in Great Britain by
Clays Ltd, St Ives plc

The Orion Publishing Group's policy is to use papers that
are natural, renewable and recyclable products and made
from wood grown in sustainable forests.The logging and
manufacturing processes are expected to conform to the
environmental regulations of the country of origin.

www.orionbooks.co.uk

For Jon, this time, with love and thanks

CONTENTS

When did it all start, the cat thing, the lion thing, the time when everything involved Cat or Leo?

With Jamie, it seemed to be the day we went to the Wildlife Park. I'd had it ages before, but that was different. I chose it. I wanted it. With Jamie, *it* chose *him*. And that had to be my fault, because I'm the one who brought it into the house with my Book and my posters and the things I collect, so maybe it started before we saw the lions. Maybe it took us a long time to notice.

1
JS ARE US

We'd always been the two Js, me and Jamie. Dad started that, ages ago when we were all together. 'How's my two Js?' he used to say, when he got in from work. But then Mum married Mike, and soon there was the new baby, making us the *three* Js – Josh, Jamie and Jennie.

Jamie and I were at the hospital, and we saw Jennie when she was about ten minutes old.

'Come and meet Jennie,' said Mike, all proud and beaming. Mum had done this before, but *he* hadn't. He was being a dad for the very first time.

Mum was sitting up in bed, holding this tiny pink thing with a screwed-up face. We both peered at it. At *her*. She looked too little to have a name at all. I didn't know how to behave. Jamie went, 'Uhhhh,' and when I tried to speak, what came out was – 'Whooowhh!' We just knew we had to whisper. It seemed wrong to talk loudly near such a small new thing. It seemed amazing that she even knew how to breathe.

Lions are the biggest African carnivores, and the largest of the big cats. They weigh two to four times as much as their cousins, the cheetah and the leopard.

'Your brand new sister,' Mike said, reaching out to touch her hand with one finger. 'Jennie. Little J.' Against the miniature baby hand, Mike's finger looked as big as a tree-trunk, and a bit grimy. He wasn't really grimy because he always showers as soon as he gets home, and comes out smelling like a peppermint, but doing all that outdoor work makes his hands rough.

'But *I'm* Little J,' said Jamie.

'Middle J now, Jamie,' Mum told him. 'You've been promoted.'

'The Three Js,' I said, quite liking it – it reminded me of the Three Musketeers, or the Three Amigos. But Jamie made a sulky face, pushing out his bottom lip.

Jennie was three days early. She was supposed to be born on December 25th. It'd be bad luck to have your birthday on Christmas Day, if you ask me – I bet you'd only get one lot of presents. But, as it turned out, Mum brought her home the day before Christmas Eve. Jamie and I decorated the tree, and Mum said it was the best ever. Nan stayed with us, to help Mum and Mike, even though Mike loves cooking and made Christmas dinner all by himself: turkey, gravy, pudding, the lot, and all Nan needed to do was set the table and put out the crackers and candles and holly decorations, and I helped with that.

Usually at Christmas we went to stay with Gran and Grandad Bryce in Bedford, but it was different this year because of Jennie. *Lots* of things were different.

We'd opened our presents as soon as we got up, but at tea-time we had little extra things from the tree – chocolate oranges or chocolate snails or chocolate money. Mum used to pretend it was the tree itself that had chosen these things and wrapped them up with our names on, and I think Jamie had only just stopped believing it. With my mouth full, I said, 'We haven't got Jennie a present! None of us did.'

'We didn't know she'd be here,' said Mum. 'And she's given *us* a present, a special one. Herself.'

'Littlest J,' Nan said. 'Our little treasure. Our best Christmas present ever.' She lifted Jennie out of Mum's arms and started talking to her in a funny cooing voice.

'You shouldn't have done it,' Jamie said. He'd twisted his shiny green chocolate wrapper into a snake, and twined it round his little finger. Everyone looked at him, and he stared back, startled, as if he'd surprised himself. 'Given her a name that starts with J,' he said.

'Why not, Jamie?' asked Mum.

'Cos Js are us,' said Jamie. 'Me and Josh.'

'Js are us?' Mike repeated. 'Sounds like a shop – Jays-R-Us!'

I laughed, but Jamie wouldn't. 'It's what Dad calls us,' he said. 'His two Js. Jennie isn't Dad's. She belongs to Mike.'

For the first time, I realised that Mike will be *Dad* to Jennie, when she learns to talk. Jamie and I don't call him that, because we've got a dad of our own. Dad's Dad, and Mike's Mike.

'She belongs to herself, Jamie,' Mum said. 'Or perhaps to all of us.'

Jamie gazed at her, then at the baby. 'Does she belong to me?' he asked.

'We belong to ourselves, and we belong to each other,' Mum said. 'All of us. That's a nice way of thinking about it.'

Mike's good at drawing, specially cartoons. Mum had tacked some of his pictures on the cork-board in the kitchen. He'd done Jamie eating porridge, going at it like a JCB digger, elbows out, sploshing gloop everywhere. He'd done Mum watering her potted plants, and he drew the kitchen windowsill to look like an Amazon rainforest. He'd done me reading a book, leaning over it as if I wanted to dive right in. And he'd done Splodge, our cat, sitting up to wash his tummy, like a big fat panda.

By bedtime on Christmas Day, Mike had done two new sketches. One was called *Jays-R-Us,* and it showed a shop-front, with two big birds perched on top. They were meant to be jays, Mike explained, with their beady eyes and strong beaks and claws. Course, I knew that, only he hadn't coloured them pink, but used ordinary pencil. In the shop window there were all sorts of things a bird might want – peanut feeders, and nesting boxes, and a dish full of wriggling worms.

The other one was called *Js are Us*. He'd drawn the three Js going up in height, like a graph. First the baby, on the ground, wrapped up in a cloth with only her face showing, like baby Jesus in a nativity play. Next came Jamie, standing proudly with his chest pushed out. Then me, tall and lanky in my Chelsea shirt. Underneath us, Mike had written *Littlest J, Middle J,* and *Biggest J.*

So I'd been promoted, too – from Big J to Biggest J. I liked it, and I didn't like it. Liked it, because it made me feel grown-up and important. Didn't like it, because it made me feel *responsible.* That was all right, if it was only when I wanted. I didn't think I could be responsible *all* the time.

Mum liked the two cartoons. Next morning they were pinned up on the kitchen cork-board.

2
Spare Room

We'd got to the time between Christmas and New Year, those odd few days that aren't special but aren't ordinary either. The weather wasn't Christmassy, but dull and wet. I stared out of the window, hoping for snow. Mike had promised to make us a bird-table, and soon I'd be able to watch birds with the binoculars I was going to buy with my Christmas present money. Jamie and I played games on the computer and read our new books and fought with each other. Brody came round and I went to his a couple of times, and we sent emails to Noori, who was with his grandparents in Lahore for the holidays. Mike was back at work, just for three days, laying hard-core for a cricket club car park in Pinner, and Nan took Jamie and me to Pizza Express and the cinema, leaving Mum at home for a rest. Then on Thursday, Jamie and I went over to Dad's, to stay till the second of January.

Dad came to pick us up. I was looking out of the window for his white van, but instead Kim was with him, and they came in Kim's red Golf.

My mum must have a thing about marrying men with white vans. Dad and Mike have both got one, but Mike's is a Transit and Dad's is a Sprinter. On the sides of Dad's it says *Paul Bryce – Painter and Decorator,* and Mike's says *Bowman Landscaping Services.* Where we lived before, we had our own driveway, and I used to look out of the front window for Dad pulling in when he got home. Here there's no drive and Mike has to park in the street, but still we look out of the window and there's a white van. And when Dad comes over in his, there's *two* white vans, with both our surnames on them, old and new. Bryce and Bowman. It's like we've jumped ship from one to the other.

Mike calls us the Bowmen. Bow*mans* sounds a bit odd, so it's his joke to say we're the Bowmen, like we're old English archers or something. (Bow*persons,* Mum says, to include her and the baby.) Mum used to be Liz Bryce, but when she married Mike she switched to Liz Bowman, and we all wondered what this meant for Jamie and me. Should we call ourselves Bowman-Bryce? Bryce-Bowman? That way we'd keep Dad's name as well as our new one, but it sounds a bit posh, and people might think we live in some huge mansion with servants and a butler, so we settled on just Bowman – 'To keep things simple,' Mum said, 'for filling in forms, and when you need passports and suchlike. Easier if we've all got the same name.'

'Except Dad,' Jamie pointed out.

'Well, yes, except Dad.'

So now we're the Bowmen, or Bowmans, or Bowpersons, and Dad's the only one who's still Bryce, unless you count Nan and Grandad. Jamie and I hardly had to change our places in the register when we changed our name. That bit was easy.

The thing I can't get used to is that when I'm with Mum, I feel as if I belong with her and Mike, and when I'm with Dad, I feel as if I belong with *him*. They're the two halves of my life. Somehow, I expect them to come together again, even though it's obvious they won't.

Lions are the most sociable of the big cats. A pride of lions can have up to fifteen females and a number of males, as well as cubs.

It was weird at first to think of someone as old as Dad having a girlfriend, but now we're used to Kim and she's basically OK. He met her about a year ago when they were doing the Three Peaks Challenge. Kim's quite easy to be with, not a fussy sort of person. She's a fitness instructor at a sports centre, and she plays football and cricket better than either of us. She never dresses up in skirts or dangly earrings or shoes she can't run fast in, like Mum sometimes does. With Kim, it's usually jeans and a sweatshirt and trainers. She always laughs a lot. At first, I thought she was younger than Mum and Dad and Mike – she looks it. But that was before we found out she's got a son, Kevin, who's a year older than me. She spends a lot of time driving Kevin to football and collecting him from his friends' houses and going to things at his school.

Course, when Dad and Kim called for us they wanted to see Jennie.

'Oh, the gorgeous little *thing*!' Kim went, so loud I'd thought she'd wake Jennie up. 'She's just adorable, Liz!'

Jennie was lying along Mum's arm, sleeping in her snuffly baby way. Now and then her mouth would open and close again, like a fish's.

'She's dreaming!' Kim said, then laughed, looking round at us all. 'But what can a tiny baby dream about?'

'She dreams about sleeping, I expect,' Dad said. 'I remember when you were like that, Jamie! No bigger than your little sister.'

Jamie looked at him, in a serious way that turned into his funny slow grin.

'Do you remember me, as well?' I asked.

Dad ruffled my hair. 'Course. Wouldn't forget that, would I?'

I looked at all of them – Mike and Mum, Dad and Kim, and Nan and the baby. It seemed there were too many of them, all standing round, with Jennie in the middle, and Jamie and me at the edges.

Mike made tea and brought out some of his special flapjack, and then it was time to go.

'OK then, Liz,' Dad said to Mum. 'See you on Monday.'

It was the last day of Nan's stay with us. She said, 'Bye then, my loveys. You take care now,' the way she always does, and we got lots of hugs and kisses on our way out of the door.

'See you next year!' Mum called out as Kim drove us

away. You'd have thought we were going away for months, instead of just three nights.

'So, what about Chelsea the other day?' Kim said, soon as we'd turned the corner and stopped waving. 'Pathetic, or what?'

'Oh no, not *football.*' Dad slumped right down in his seat and pretended to be sleeping. 'Wake me up when you've finished.' He didn't really hate football all that much, but he always pretended to when the three of us started on about it.

We left London, and headed for the M40. On the way I saw signs pointing to Hillingdon, which is where we lived when we were all together. After our old house was sold, we moved further into London, and Dad moved further out. He'd only just got his new place, in High Wycombe, so we hadn't seen it yet.

Outside the M25 there were fields and woods and glimpses of river, and soon we saw houses and streets spreading over a hillside.

'Is this countryside?' Jamie asked.

'High Wycombe's quite a big town,' Dad told him. 'But we're right on the edge, and there's plenty of countryside around us. I thought we'd go to the Cotswold Wildlife Park tomorrow.'

'Boss!' said Jamie. This was something he'd started saying lately, picked up from his friend Arran.

Kim caught my eye in the driving mirror and gave me a puzzled look, so I translated for her. 'He means *cool.* Cotswold Wildlife? What, foxes and deer and badgers?'

'No,' said Dad. 'It's more like a zoo.'

'Big cats?' I said quickly.

'Oh yes, I checked that. You can look at the website when we get in.'

Dad's house was bigger than ours, and newer. Most of the front garden was taken up with driveway, big enough for Kim's car and Dad's van. Inside, everything was tidy – there were no Christmas decorations like ours at home, no tree, just some cards strung up and a few candles on the mantelpiece. It looked a bit bare. The back garden was twice the size of ours, with trees and a bird-table and a bat-box and a log-pile for toads to shelter in.

'Typical of your dad,' Kim joked. 'He hasn't got curtains in all the rooms yet, but he's got a bat-box.'

'I'm going to dig a pond in the summer,' Dad told us. 'You can help, if you like. Every garden needs a pond, and a boggy area. Then we'll start to get frogs and dragonflies, maybe even newts.'

He showed us round indoors, downstairs and up. There was a bedroom specially for me and Jamie, with bunk beds, and there was Dad's room, and a very small study with a lot of boxes waiting to be unpacked. There was the bathroom, and another door that Dad hadn't opened.

'What's in there?' I asked.

He showed us. It was another bedroom with a single bed in it and a TV and a desk, but not much else.

'Whose is that?' Jamie demanded.

'Er – well, it's spare, for now,' Dad said.

'Do you live here as well?' Jamie asked Kim.

She went a bit red. 'No. Just stay sometimes. Me and Kevin live in Aylesbury, not far away.'

There was something going on here I didn't want to know about. The spare room wasn't Kim's, that was obvious, only Jamie was too young to know. There were no bags in there, or clothes. But in Dad's room – he'd only shown us quickly – I'd seen a cream dressing-gown and some fleece slippers that were too small for Dad. All I thought, at first, was that Jamie and I could have had a room each. I mean, why keep a bedroom empty, if there's no one to use it? We had to share at home, because the third bedroom, the small one, was going to be Jennie's.

Then it struck me. That room was for Kevin. He'd be staying here as well, wouldn't he? He was at his nan's at the moment, Kim had told us. If not for that he'd be here now. He'd be here whenever Kim came to stay.

I didn't like that. Kevin's room. Kevin was having a room to himself, in Dad's house. Why hadn't Dad *said*?

But I wasn't going to let Kevin spoil the end of the year, specially as he wasn't even here. As soon as I could get on the computer, I checked out the Cotswold Wildlife Park website and found that they had Asiatic Lions and Amur Leopards. Also White-lipped Peccaries, Yellow Mongooses (or is it Mongeese?), Reticulated Pythons and Scimitar-Horned Oryx. It looked good.

'Have a look at this, Jame,' I said. 'Here's what we'll see tomorrow.' But he was watching TV, so he only had a quick look.

He was still normal Jamie, then. As far as anyone could tell.

But next day, he saw the lion. And the lion saw him.

3
CATS' EYES

The wildlife park was enormous. There were camels and zebras, reptiles and rhinos. There was a tropical house full of steamy indoor jungle, where birds, all brilliant colours, flitted about in the leaves so close that the air from their wingtips brushed my ears. There were spider monkeys, leaping from branch to branch and swinging on ropes. There were two Vietnamese pot-bellied pigs, fast asleep on a bed of straw, snoring loudly.

Kim giggled and prodded Dad in the ribs. 'Now who do they remind me of?'

'Mike snores, too,' Jamie told Dad. 'Only not as loud as you.'

It was so cold that I quite fancied snuggling in the straw with those pigs. My breath clouded in front of my face and I had to keep wiggling my toes inside my boots to keep them warm. But the cold was making the day special. It was that crisp, bright kind of cold – the grass crunched as we walked on it, and the low sun dazzled.

Best of all were the lions. There was a family of them,

out in the sunshine in a grass enclosure. We stood together, Jamie huddled against Dad's legs, and watched the lions through a big pane of glass that was built into the fence. The lioness lay with her twin cubs on a mound, while the male prowled and prowled, walking in a slack, powerful way, his eyes swivelling. He'd worn a path beside a deep ditch that ran all the way round the enclosure, just inside the fence.

'Patrolling his territory,' Kim said. 'Keeping an eye on things.'

'Both eyes,' said Jamie.

I realised how close the lion would come as he padded along the ditch below us. Excitement shivered through me. I stood perfectly still, but he didn't look up. As he passed, I stared down at his rough, shaggy mane, and his tawny fur. What would it be like to push my hands into that thick mane, and feel his hot lion breath? I could smell him, strong and catty. I was close to a real lion, *incredibly* close, near enough to reach down and touch him if the glass pane hadn't been there. Jamie pressed himself back against Dad's legs. He must have stopped breathing, because I heard him let out a gust of air as the lion padded on past.

The female didn't move from her mound. She was clasping a bloody chunk of bone, big enough to be from a cow or a pig. She held it down with one paw, licking it.

'Did she kill it?' said Jamie. 'That bone?'

Kim huffed a laugh.

'No, J,' said Dad, tugging at the zip on Jamie's fleece. 'The park-keepers gave it to them. They don't have to kill, not here.'

The cubs were playing around the lioness, rolling and

tumbling and batting, like kittens. When one of them tried to tug at the bone, she gave it a cuff with her big front paw.

'She won't hurt it, will she?' said Jamie.

'Oh no,' Dad told him. 'She's just saying, *this is mine – keep off*. She won't hurt her own cubs.'

'Not like Splodge with that mouse!' I reminded Jamie. 'Remember how fierce he was?'

About two weeks before, Splodge brought a mouse into the front room, where we were all watching TV. Mum let out a shriek and Mike sprang to his feet, but Splodge backed off, with a strange low growl in his throat. I was nearer. I got down on the floor and tried to work out how to save the mouse. If I pulled it away, Splodge would grip tighter with his teeth. Its eyes made me think of apple-pips, and its pink paws were like hands as it dangled from Splodge's mouth. Splodge's eyes glared with an angry wildness I'd never seen before – usually, he was a big softie. The mouse made a tiny sound, too tiny even to be a squeak, more like a gasp. Its front paws twitched feebly, and then, all in a second, I saw it die. The light went out of its eyes, and it hung quite still from Splodge's jaws, a limp, dead thing.

I saw then how mysterious a life is. How, when it flickers out, nothing can bring it back.

'What, did daft old Splodge-Puss manage to catch a mouse?' Dad said now. 'I'm surprised he could be bothered to heave himself off the sofa!'

'He killed it!' Jamie said proudly.

At the time, he'd been more excited than upset. I'd only thought how terrified the mouse must have been. And of that tiny, quick, heartbeating life, crushed to nothing.

'Can you smell lion?' I said. 'I can. It's strong and catty and furry. That's why lions have to get downwind of whatever they're stalking.'

Dad sniffed. 'You must have a good sense of smell. I can only smell mud and grass.'

'I can,' said Jamie, still clinging to Dad's coat. 'I can smell lion.'

'How about that?' Kim said. 'I wonder how many people can say they've been so close to a real live lion? I took Kevin to Whipsnade a couple of years ago, but we didn't get as close as this.'

'Would he attack us if the fence wasn't there?' Jamie asked.

Dad shook his head. 'I don't know. And I'm glad we won't be finding out.'

The lion broke away from his circuit and loped to the top of the mound. He only glanced at the female and cubs, then stood with his head high, taking in smells and sounds from across the park. Dad passed me his binoculars, and as I focused, the lion turned his heavy head and looked straight at me with his amber eyes. A shock fizzled through me. I couldn't look away from those stern, solemn lion eyes – I was held there, staring and staring back at him. For that second, there was nothing between me and him – no binoculars, no glass panel, no fence. I felt sure he knew me, knew what I was thinking.

Then he turned away.

'Here, Dad.' I handed back the binoculars, and he offered them to Kim. Jamie had slunk round behind Dad.

Kim laughed. 'It's all right, Jame. He can't get you.'

'The fence isn't all that high.' From behind Dad, Jamie

tilted his head at it. 'I bet a lion could jump that if he wanted.'

'Not with the ditch underneath,' Dad told him. 'The park-keepers must know what they're doing.'

The lion stared in another direction for a few moments, then gave a sigh and lay down near the lioness.

'Now he's like one of the lions in Trafalgar Square,' Kim said.

We stood looking a bit longer. Kim took a couple of photos with the camera Dad had given her for Christmas. My fingers were going numb, and Jamie was stamping his feet to keep warm.

'I don't like seeing lions in cages,' Dad said.

'Hey!' Kim jabbed his arm. 'It was your idea to come!'

'Yeah, I know,' said Dad. 'I don't mind it so much with monkeys or deer. But lions – it doesn't seem right.'

'Oh, they look quite happy to me.' Kim was looking at the leaflet with the map of the park. 'It's what they're used to.'

I wasn't sure. I'd wanted to come here, to see the lions and leopards in particular, but now I saw what Dad meant. It didn't seem right for them to be penned up for people to stare at. Suddenly I felt ashamed of staring through binoculars. There was something about that lion that couldn't be penned up in a cage. Something fierce and free.

'*I* like them in cages,' Jamie said. 'It's better than having them roam around wherever they want.'

Kim tugged at the brim of his woolly hat so that it went right down over his eyebrows. 'Lions don't live wild in this country, Jamie! They come from Africa.'

'I know *that*!' He pulled away, and pushed the hat out of his eyes. 'I was just *supposing*.'

I just had to put Kim right. 'These aren't African lions,' I told her. 'They're Asiatic. They're from India, from the Gir Forest in Gujurat.'

She could have read that for herself on the notice-board, but I'd already worked out that she was the sort of person who said things without really knowing if they were true or not. Then I remembered something I'd read in the *Wildlife of Africa* book Dad gave me for Christmas. 'D'you know how people first learned to be safe from lions?'

'When they made guns?' said Jamie.

'No! Before that. Ages before guns.'

'When they made zoos?' Jamie tried.

'No! Ages before that, as well.'

'Go on then, Josh,' said Dad. 'Tell us.' We started to walk away from the lions, towards some camels that stood in a bored, sniffy group outside their shed.

'It was when they learned to make fire,' I said. 'Back in the Stone Age. Before, they could only hide in their caves and hope the lions wouldn't find them. But once they learned to make fire, they were much safer.'

'How?' said Jamie.

I thought he meant how did early humans learn to make fire, and I was about to explain how they must have got the idea from seeing trees struck by lightning, but Kim told him, 'The lions would have been frightened off by the flames.'

Jamie frowned. 'I didn't think a lion would be frightened.'

'Survival instinct. They know how not to get hurt.' Dad looked at his watch. 'Come on – only another hour till closing. I'm freezing, I don't know about you lot. *My*

Facts & Figures

Cats are active at night and in the dusk, so they have to be able to see well without much light. They can see in one-sixth of the light humans need. But their eyes have to work in bright daylight as well.

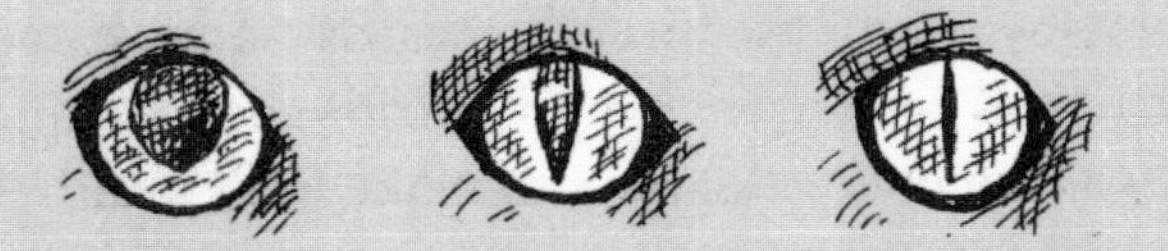

In bright light, the pupil shrinks to a small slit, but in darkness it opens very wide. A cat's eye is relatively bigger than a human's, so more light can be let in. The back of a cat's eye is like a mirror, reflecting, to make the most of low light. That's why you see a cat's eyes glowing in headlights. Human eyes don't do that.

survival instinct's telling me to get inside a nice warm building.'

We headed for the insect house and the fruit bats. We finished up in the shop, where I chose some postcards for my Book of Cats. Jamie bought a puzzle, and Kim bought a lion key-ring for herself and a disposable camera for Kevin.

It was already dark by the time we set off home. Kim drove, Dad sat next to her with the map, Jamie with me in the back. Our headlamps lit up the string of lights, one by one, that showed us the middle of the country road.

'Cats' eyes,' Jamie said suddenly. 'They only come on at night, don't they? Who switches them on?'

I gave him a little shove. 'Durr! You really think someone goes round turning cats' eyes on, along miles and miles of roads? Each one with its own little switch?'

'They're reflectors, Jamie,' Dad said over his shoulder. 'It's the light from our headlamps, shining back. Clever idea – I wonder who thought of it?'

'So why are they called cats' eyes?' Jamie asked.

'Because cats can see in the dark,' Kim explained.

'No! Because cats' eyes *reflect* in the dark,' I corrected her. 'You've seen that, Jamie, haven't you? When we had our torches on bonfire night, and saw Splodge by the hedge.'

'That's right, Josh,' Dad said. 'Cats' eyes are different from ours.'

I thought about lions and fire and darkness. I saw a bright bonfire, with flames snapping and leaping, sparks lifting into

the dark. A circle of faces, golden with firelight. People sitting, huddled into their furs and skins, thinking they were safe. And they would be safe for as long as the fire burned, but behind them in the blackness there would be crouched shapes. There would be amber lion eyes watching, waiting.

4
THE BOOK OF CATS

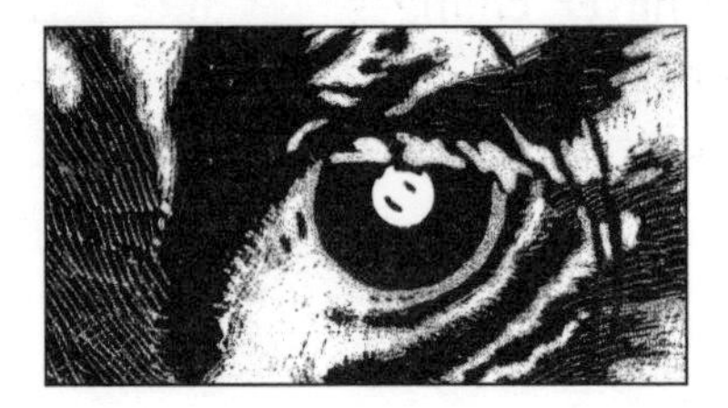

I don't know what it is with cats and me. I've been fascinated by them ever since I was little. Lions, leopards and tigers, cheetahs and ocelots. Ordinary cats as well. So I suppose it must have started with Mister, who was our cat till he had to be put to sleep. This was a long time ago, when Mum and Dad were together, but Mister's still a sort of legend in our family. Mister the Magnificent, we called him. It was Dad who thought of the name Mister, because of the M-pattern Mister had on his forehead. He was a special cat, and he knew it. The way he paraded about, you could tell he thought he was king of the street. He had a few scars, from battles he'd fought with cats who thought they could take him on.

There's something about cats and lions that pulls me to them. It's not just how beautiful they are. It's not just the gleam of their eyes or the way they stare. It's not just their sleek fur or the pad of their feet or the ways they move. What it is – I don't know what to call it except spirit of cat. Spirit of cat is in all of them, and it's been there for hundreds – no, thousands – of years. What goes on in a lion's head must be the same as it ever was. They might live in the twenty-first century and be kept in Wildlife Parks and have their pictures taken with digital cameras, but lion spirit never changes. It's like a deep fire that's been smouldering since ancient times and will go on smouldering as long as there are lions in the world. I hope that's forever.

Another thing I like, you can keep lions in cages and zoos and even circuses, but you can't tame them. Even house cats – Mum says they live with us on their own terms. 'You can own a dog,' she says, 'but a cat owns you.' Often it *chooses* you. That's what happened with Mister, before Jamie and I were even born. He turned up in the garden one day, and soon he seemed to be there all the time, and next thing he'd moved in. Mum and Dad tried to find out whose cat he was, but no one ever claimed him and he decided to stay.

Even a fat, soft thing like Splodge, who spends half the day sleeping – he's still made of spirit of cat, and he stares at you sometimes to let you know it. His eyes are green and deep, and it's like he can see into my mind. He can see whatever's in there.

He stares the stare of all cats. Proud and strong, knowing exactly what it is. Cat.

It was from Gran that I got the idea of the Book of Cats. That's Gran Bryce, Dad's mum.

When we go to Gran and Grandad's, she shows us how she's getting on with her Book of the Seasons, her special scrapbook. She starts a new one every year. *She* got the idea from this old book she's got, *The Country Diary of an Edwardian Lady,* full of sketches and notes. When the Edwardian Lady noticed anything – the first primrose, when the first swallows arrived, stuff like that – she wrote it down in her book, and did a drawing. Gran liked the book so much, she decided to start her own. Now, every Christmas, Dad gives her a new notebook – a big one with hard covers, like a proper book – and she decorates the front with a collage of pictures cut from birthday cards and magazines, so each one's different. In them she keeps cuttings and poems and notes. She writes in calligraphy pen (she learned to do that specially) and she does little pictures of flowers and fields and the birds that come to her bird table. She's not much good at drawing, to be honest, but she colours them in nicely and labels them and does borders of ivy or violets or snowflakes. Each book goes through a whole year, from the birds in the garden on January 1st to the berries left on the trees by the end of December.

She's got eight of them now, on the top shelf of her bookcase. Dad calls them her Works of Art.

He says it's from Gran and Grandad that I get my love of wildlife. They've got a garden with trees and a bird-table, not just a square of grass like ours. Grandad puts out bread and seed every day, and he taught me which birds are which. Since I was little, I've been able to tell a greenfinch from a chaffinch, and a jackdaw from a rook, and a coal-tit from a blue tit. So can Jamie, and Dad's even better, because he can recognise birds from their calls. Sometimes we're walking through trees and he'll suddenly go, 'Listen! Green woodpecker,' and we'll stop and look round and sometimes see a flash of green.

Anyway, last Christmas I decided to make a Book of Cats. Dad bought me a really good notebook, a set of felt pens, and glue. It's a kind of project. Anything to do with cats, anything I like, goes into that book – bits of information from the internet, postcards, pictures from magazines. And lots of facts. I like facts, because you put them into your brain and they stay there even when you forget them, and sometimes come out all by themselves.

My Book of Cats is my special place. It's mine and I know what's in it. It's like I can get right inside it and not come out till I want to.

The cover's a collage, like Gran's book. At first I started with anything I could find – lion and tiger photos, a Leo zodiac sign, a tiger mask, a Chinese lion made of bronze. But the thing with a collage is you can keep adding to it, and I've added and added to mine till the front cover is thick and padded. What it's got now is eyes – cat eyes, lion eyes, tiger eyes, all these pairs of bright eyes, staring and staring. It's amazing how many pairs of eyes you can find, once you start looking.

The Book of Cats stays on the desk in our bedroom, and I look at it or add something or do a new drawing nearly every day. It's mine, and I never show it to anyone apart from family. Even Brody and Noori don't know about it. The only time it leaves the house is when I stay with Dad, because he likes seeing what's new, and he's always got lots of books and magazines like *National Geographic*, so I might find something good.

My other rule is no cartoons. No Tom and Jerry, no Lion King, no Disney Jungle Book. I don't like cats turned into cartoon jokes. I like them real.

5 RED KITES

'What're we doing tomorrow?' Jamie asked, when we'd had tea. It was pizza, chips and ice-cream, from the freezer. Dad and Kim aren't into cooking the way Mike is.

'Well, it's New Year's Eve,' Dad said. 'And we always do something special on the last day of the year.'

With Dad, *something special* usually means going to a nature reserve or out for a long walk. The year before, it was bird-watching at Minsmere. It was ear-achingly cold in the East wind that cut in from the sea, the sort of cold that goes right through your clothes and makes you think you'll never warm up again. We sat in the hide with our sandwiches and flask, and I got so frozen that my legs were numbed in position and my hands could hardly hold the binoculars. But we saw little egrets and a marsh harrier and a whole flock of wintering Brent geese, so it was worth it.

'Yes. And?' went Jamie.

'I thought we'd go for a walk on the Ridgeway,' Dad

said. 'Specially if it's as bright as today. We'll probably see red kites. There are lots of them, up on the Chilterns.'

'Cool!' said Jamie.

Dad looked at Kim. 'And, um, I think Kevin's coming. Is that right, Kim?'

The cat family is felidae. All organisms in the world have a Latin name so that it doesn't matter what language you start from, the scientific name is always the same. So humans are homo sapiens. Sometimes the names are quite easy to remember, like bumble bee is bombus bombus, and wren is troglodytes troglodytes. Big name for a very small bird. And the thrush family is called turdus. I'm not making that up. Turdus viscivorus is mistle thrush, and turdus philomelos is song thrush. Back to cats, the domestic cat is felis catus, which is why so many cats are called Felix, as well as Felix cat food.

'Yes,' said Kim, stacking the dishwasher. 'Mum's dropping him off around nine.'

Right, I thought, and I bet he'll be staying here. In that bedroom.

'It's nice for you boys to have each other's company,' Kim told us.

Kevin turned up while we were having breakfast. His nan brought him, and stayed for coffee. We'd met Kevin three or four times before, and he was always the same. He was a good bit taller than me, and he wore a peaked cap and a baggy sweatshirt and baggy jeans and trainers. His dull, bored expression showed he'd rather be somewhere else, and he was one of those people who talk without moving their face, like they can't spare the energy.

We said hello to Kevin, and he went *Ur.* His eyes flicked towards us then away, to show he hadn't seen anything worth bothering with. He reminded me of Toby at school, who thinks he's hard.

'Boys, this is my mum,' said Kim. 'Kevin's nan.'

'Pleased to meet you, Josh and Jamie,' said the nan, who was a smiley sort of person like Kim. Smileyness in their family must have run out when it reached Kevin.

Course, Dad had to go all breezy and embarrassing, coming out with things like, 'Well! It's a good day for it!' and 'Be a bit bracing up on those hills,' and even, 'Get Josh to tell you about the Wildlife Park, Kev.'

Kevin said nothing to any of this. He said nothing at all, even when Kim or his nan spoke to him, and then he only said 'Uh,' without looking at anyone. I ate my toast. Jamie drank his milk. Dad's jolliness, and Kevin's silence, made me want to be anywhere but here.

At last Kevin's nan left, and we were ready to go. Dad drove us out of town and along narrow lanes that wound up through beech woods to a car park. We got out and gathered round the car boot, putting on wellies and scarves and hats and gloves and coats. Kevin stood waiting. He hadn't brought a jacket, or anything else. He stood with his hands shoved into the pockets of his hoodie.

'Sure you don't want a coat, Kev?' Dad asked again – he'd tried to lend him one before we left the house.

'Nuh,' went Kevin, scuffing his trainer on the stony ground.

We set off. The path led along a dried-leaf track, rustly under our feet, then opened out to downland – there was a grassy slope plunging away, and fields and roads and villages spreading out for miles and miles. We were looking all the way to Oxford, Dad said, pointing, and the towers of Didcot Power Station. We saw blue hills to the north, and all the land laid out in the sunshine – a tiny tractor ploughing a field, and two people riding horses. It was fantastic! Being up so high made me feel small and unimportant, but also big and strong, as if my feet could carry me for miles and miles, the whole length of the Ridgeway.

'Did you know,' I said, 'the Ridgeway's 85 miles long, but that's only the marked bit? Once it was probably much longer than that. It's one of the oldest green roads in Europe. It goes back to the Bronze Age at least.'

I'd looked it up on the internet last night. I like learning new facts. I thought of us walking where people had trudged along hundreds and even thousands of years ago, with their pack mules, with things to sell or trade.

'Walking encyclopaedia, you are!' Kim tweaked the end of my scarf.

And, exactly as Dad had promised, we saw red kites – five of them! First there were four, circling and swooping over a clump of trees below us. With the binoculars, we got a really good look, and heard them calling in that way that sends a shiver of excitement through me. They're streamlined and perfect, climbing the air, riding the wind. You could easily think they're showing off, but they don't need to show off because flying's what they do, what they're made for. The light was so good that I saw the reddish-brown of their wings and tails, the white wing-patches and the black primary feathers that stretch out like fingers. Later, we saw one on its own, even closer – it had landed on a ploughed field, but took off when it saw us. Just lifted itself into the air, and glided away over the trees.

'What, they're the kites you're all on about?' Kevin said, the first time he'd spoken in actual words. 'Them birds?'

Dad would have corrected me or Jamie, with '*Those* birds,' but he didn't correct Kevin.

'Oh, sorry, Kev!' Kim laughed and gave him a big hug, not seeming to notice that he just put up with it and waited for her to stop. 'You must have thought we meant people flying kites on strings! Well, they do that here as well. We might see some in a bit.'

Kevin shrugged, to show it was all just as boring to him. I could have gone 'Duh!' – I bet he would, if I said something stupid – but Dad was looking at me with a kind of warning, so I kept quiet.

We stood looking a bit longer. I thought of the amazing

eyesight of a bird of prey, acute enough to see a vole or a mouse from on high. I thought of it scanning the landscape from a current of air, seeing woods and hills and valleys, not the roads and towns that human maps are made of. I thought of the freedom of having the whole sky to float in.

'Brilliant!' said Dad. He offered his binoculars to Kevin. 'Want these? You'd be lucky to get a better view than this!'

Kevin shook his head. 'Nuh. Seen it.'

Dad stood there puzzled, still holding out the binoculars. He's so keen on birdwatching that he can't see why everyone else isn't. That's one of the things he and Mum used to argue about – Mum could never understand why Dad wanted to go haring off to the Ouse Washes or Romney Marsh or the Isles of Scilly any time he got the chance. 'To spend all day standing in a swamp? Not my idea of a weekend away.' So Dad went, and Mum stayed at home. Now Dad could go whenever he wanted. Kim didn't seem the sort of person who'd stop him doing what he wanted.

'Kevin's not much into birds, are you?' said Kim. 'But they're incredible, those kites. So big! Where do they nest?'

'Here,' I told her, 'in trees. They used to be really rare. You'd have had to go to south Wales to see them, once. But they've been released here and it's worked really well. There are supposed to be two hundred and something breeding pairs in the Chilterns, and they're spreading.'

Kim stared at me. 'The things you know! How do you do it?'

I shrugged. 'Dunno. I read stuff, and remember.'

'Well, it's totally amazing! Isn't it, Kevin?'

'Kuh,' went Kevin.

It's embarrassing, this sort of thing. I mean, why should anyone be surprised? Facts are everywhere – the only way *not* to find them would be to walk around with your eyes and ears shut. I'm lucky, Mum says, to have such a good memory. But I know that some people at school think I'm a nerd for knowing stuff and remembering things. That's why I usually keep quiet in class. When I'm with Mum or Mike or Dad, though, they like me coming out with interesting facts, specially Dad.

When we moved off, Kevin came up close behind me and said in my ear, in a parroty squawk, *'Did you know? Did you know?* No, I didn't,' he went on, dropping his voice, 'and you know what? I couldn't give a toss. Duh!'

He'd got me down as a geeky know-all, too. So I don't know why I carried on, but I did. '*Milvus milvus,* that's the red kite's Latin name.'

Kevin rolled his eyes. I took no notice. The last day of the year ought to be a good one if you ask me, and it was great up here. If he wanted to trail along looking grumpy, that was up to him. But when I noticed that Jamie was lagging behind as well, I stopped to wait.

'That was boss, wasn't it?' I said to him. 'The kites? Did you get a good look?'

'Yes,' he said. 'Only I don't like their eyes.'

'Don't be soft! They're not going to swoop down on you. They eat mainly dead things, anyway – carrion. And you couldn't have seen their eyes, not at that range.'

'I did, though,' he insisted. 'They stare like lions. Only they didn't talk to me. The lion did.'

'The lion talked to you? What are you on about?'

'He did,' Jamie said in a small voice. 'He talked to me. He told me something.'

'Oh, yeah? And what was that?'

'I forget,' said Jamie.

Something made me turn round. There was Kevin, close behind us, with a smirky little grin on his face that made me want to hit him.

6
JAMIE'S DREAM

'I need to explain something,' Dad said. 'The thing is, Js, next time you come to stay, Kim will have moved in as well.'

We were in the van, going home. It was New Year now, January the second. We'd stayed up to see the New Year in, Dad and Jamie and me – not Kim, because she'd left with Kevin so that he could go to a party. So the three of us had jacket potatoes and cheese and beans for dinner, and watched a film, and played this game Dad had got for us called Dingbats, and tried to stay awake (Jamie failed, but we woke him up for Big Ben) and it was just the way I liked it.

But now this.

'What d'you mean, moved in?' I said. 'I thought she had her own house.'

'She's selling it,' Dad explained. 'There've been a few hitches with her buyer, but the sale's going through now. So she'll be moving all her stuff in. The week after next, we hope.'

'All her stuff?' I repeated. Then it dawned on me. 'You mean Kevin?'

'Er, yes.' Dad was waiting to pull out at a roundabout. 'He'll have to change schools – it'll be tough for him, halfway through Year 8.'

Jamie was sitting between us, and I didn't think he'd been listening properly, but he had. 'Kevin? Kevin's going to live at your house?' He was almost yelling in Dad's ear. 'You're having Kevin instead of us?'

'No, no, boys, it's not like that,' said Dad. 'It's not only my house, see – it's mine and Kim's. We've bought it together. She had to get a bridging loan.'

I imagined wads of banknotes like bricks, glued together in a huge arc, bridging the gap between Kim's house and Dad's.

'So, what, does that mean you'll get married, then?' I asked. 'Like Mum and Mike?'

'Well, we might. Only that's a way off – we'll get Kim moved in first. Look, I'm not doing this very well, am I? We'll stop at Burger King. There's one along here.'

So we stopped, and ordered burgers and milkshakes for me and Jamie, but Dad only had coffee. He talked, and I listened, and Jamie concentrated on stuffing himself. Dad went on and on about changes, and moving on, and it was difficult for us but he knew we'd adjust, and he was making a new life with Kim, and Kevin was part of that, but we had our own room and we could come as often as we wanted. He told us we'll always be very very very extra-special to him because we're his Js and he loves us, and that's one thing that will never change.

'Yeah, OK, Dad.' I was embarrassed by this kind of talk.

Jamie hadn't quite finished his burger, but he pushed it away and leaned back in his seat. 'Can we go now? I want to go home.'

When we got in, Dad didn't stay long – he had to go back and sort out his van for work next day. Just a quick chat with Mum and Mike, and more about the baby, and some Happy New Yearing. Then he was gone, saying he'd see us the weekend after next. 'And we'll get your new binoculars then,' he told me. 'I promise.'

We stood on the pavement and waved as he drove away.

So that's it, I thought. Me and Jamie with Dad, properly together for the last time. It won't be the same any more, with Kim and Kevin in the way. Dad'll be with them. They'll get more of him than we will.

Moving on, he says. Right. Moving on from the Js to the Ks. Leaving us behind.

In England

black cats are thought to be lucky and some people think white cats are unlucky. But in America it's the other way round.

I suppose the start of the year should feel bright and new, but instead it felt like standing on the edge of something I couldn't see. I didn't know yet what sort of year it would be, what would happen, what might be waiting. I wasn't sure yet whether this New Year felt safe to live in.

For a second, in the dizziness of waking up, I thought it was me that had yelled. The sound echoed in my ears – a cry of terror, suddenly choked off. Then I heard Jamie whimpering, and realised it was him.

I fumbled for the switch and clicked the bedside lamp on. 'Jamie?'

For a few seconds I'd thought we were still at Dad's, till our own room came into focus. Dark blue curtains, my leopard poster, our football scarves looped over the back of the chair, books and CDs on the desk. Everything looked normal except Jamie. He was huddled in his duvet, sobbing.

'Jame?'

I swung my feet to the floor, leaned over to his bed and touched his shoulder. He made an angry sound and hunched himself away from me. Then Mum came in, pulling her dressing-gown round her, tying the belt.

'Josh? What's going on?'

'It's Jamie,' I said. 'He's had a nightmare or something.'

Mum sat on his bed and cuddled him, going *shh-shh-shh* the way she did with the baby. I sat watching, with my duvet round me, a big padded cloak. Jamie was crying like a little kid, the sobs catching at his breath like hiccups. Gradually, with the *shhh*ing, his sobs calmed and he lay quietly in Mum's arms. I could see his eyes open, his eyelashes wet with tears. I picked up Lowther, his bear, who'd slid to the floor, and sat him on Jamie's pillow. Jamie didn't say a word.

'What was it, little J?' Mum asked. 'Bad dream?'

Jamie nodded and closed his eyes.

'What did you dream?' Mum asked gently.

'Can't remember,' Jamie said, in a baby whimper.

Mum looked at me.

'He yelled out, really yelled!' I told her. 'I nearly went through the roof. Then he started crying.'

Jamie pushed Mum away, wriggled out of bed and started putting socks on, his new Chelsea ones. 'Can I have cocoa?' he asked in a perfectly normal voice.

From Mum and Mike's room, we heard the thin wail of the baby starting to cry, then a grunt from Mike and a creaking of the mattress.

Mum sighed. 'Now we're *all* awake. I'll fetch Jennie in here, and perhaps Mike'll make us all a hot drink.' She stood up and tugged Jamie's duvet straight.

'And jackflap,' Jamie called after her as she left. 'Is there some left?'

He was wide awake now. I really thought he'd made up the nightmare just to get cocoa and flapjack at one o'clock in the morning.

'What's this, a midnight feast?' Mike grumbled, looking in on his way downstairs. I heard him open the kitchen door, then give a muffled yelp, followed by a *burr*-ing sound and quick cat feet on the stairs. Splodge. Splodge was good at tripping people up in the dark. He arrived in our room, tail high, pleased with himself. After he'd walked slowly round my bed, he jumped up on Jamie's. He rolled over and looked up at Jamie, wanting his tummy stroked.

'Get off,' Jamie said, and shoved him quite roughly. Splodge gave a *yaow* of complaint, and caught at the duvet with his claws.

'Don't be mean!' I reached out to Splodge and lifted him on to my bed. Once he'd unhuffed himself from being pushed, he snuggled up to me, purring. If he got right down under the duvet, he might get away with spending the rest of the night there, instead of in his basket in the kitchen. I liked having him with me, like a furry hot-water bottle. I liked the smell of his fur and his warm cat breath when he yawned, and the pads of his paws that were cool then warm when you pressed them, and his claws that curved so neat and smooth. He was silly old Splodge, but also perfectly Cat.

'I don't want him,' Jamie whined. 'Take him away!'

Usually Jamie and I argue about who's going to have him, and whoever's bed Splodge chooses thinks he's the lucky one, the favourite. But Mum's rule is No Cats in Bedrooms, specially not in beds. And now that we've got the baby, Splodge isn't even supposed to come upstairs. If she sees a suspicious bulge under the duvet, Mum hoicks him out.

'I want Lowther,' Jamie insisted. 'Not Splodge.'

'No problem, then. You've *got* Lowther.'

Splodge burrowed under the duvet, next to me, and his throaty purring seemed to spread through my own body.

Jamie's voice went babyish again. 'No! I don't want him in here! Take him down!'

Now Mum was back, carrying the incredibly noisy bundle that was our baby sister. Jennie wasn't going to let us forget she was here. Loud wails pumped out of her with barely a pause for breath.

'Is that cat in there?' Mum peered suspiciously at the bulge by my legs. 'You know the rule! OUT, Splodge!'

Balancing the baby, she flipped my duvet over, and out streaked Splodge. Jamie settled back, clutching Lowther, looking triumphant at getting his own way. Couldn't have been that scary a nightmare, I thought, if he'd forgotten it already.

Only of course he hadn't.

7
CAT GOT YOUR TONGUE?

I like school, really, and it would be good seeing Brody and Noori. All the same, it was an effort to drag myself out of holiday mood and get back into the routine – packing my school bag, reminding myself which lessons we'd have and whether I'd done my homework. First day back it was Maths, English, double Science, French and PE.

St Luke's Juniors is on the same site as my school, Langtree High, with a fence and a gate in between. Mum likes me to walk Jamie to school and collect him on the way back, unless she's coming herself. Arran – he's Jamie's best friend – waits for us at the corner of Harcourt Drive, and usually we meet Noori and Brody by the paper shop, so all I do is keep Jamie in sight and make sure we cross the main road together. On the way home, though, there's ten minutes to wait outside St Luke's, because the juniors finish a bit later than we do. Brody has to collect his little sister, and most days Noori comes too. That time of day, there's this gaggle of mums and toddlers and buggies and the odd dad or grandad waiting outside the juniors, so we hang back by the play area and this little garden they've made, with a pond and a bridge.

Sometimes, Mr Rose comes over to talk to us. When *we* were at St Luke's he took our class for year 5 and year 6, so we know him quite well.

Everyone likes Mr Rose. He runs the football team, and organises all the matches. Mum jokes that he looks about eighteen, with his short spiked hair and his sports gear. Noori and Brody and I used to be in his team, so sometimes when he comes out we have a chat about fixtures or how Chelsea are doing, or how we're getting on at Langtree. Quite often he doesn't speak to us at all, because parents often want to talk to him, but he always gives us a nod and a wave.

That first day back, though, he seemed to be looking for us. He came straight over.

'Josh?' he called. 'I hoped I'd catch you. I'm a bit worried about Jamie – I don't think he's well.'

'Oh? What's wrong?' I asked. Jamie had seemed perfectly all right when we walked to school in the morning.

I followed him in through the side door. Noori and Brody waited outside.

'He hasn't spoken all day,' Mr Rose told me. 'Not a single word. Has he got a sore throat, lost his voice?'

'Not this morning he hadn't.' I tried to think back as far as breakfast. We'd all been there, all four of us – I mean all five, counting Jennie in her crib. Jamie had talked then, I was sure – we'd all have noticed if he hadn't. Yes, I remembered now. Mike had this new coffee machine he'd bought in the sales, that foamed the milk with a great hissing of steam. He was going, 'You like-a, ah? Espresso splendido for the lovely *señora*.' And Mum said, 'That makes the coffee taste better. Definitely.' Then Mike taught Jamie and me to count up to ten in Italian, and we'd chanted the numbers together as we walked along our street. *Una, duo, tre, quattro, cinque* . . . They were nice words to say.

'Yes, he was counting in Italian,' I told Mr Rose. 'Mike started teaching us. You know, our stepdad.'

'He's not from Italy, is he?'

'No, from Leighton Buzzard.'

'And did Jamie speak in English as well?'

'Yes! He seemed perfectly OK.'

'He didn't say anything about feeling unwell? Having a sore throat?'

I shook my head.

'He's not said a single word since he got here, not even to Arran, not even to answer his name in the register.' Mr Rose looked at me anxiously. 'Was he upset about coming back to school after the holiday?'

I shook my head. 'Don't think so.'

'And he's not been ill over Christmas and New Year?'

'No!'

We were in the corridor now. I could see the open door to my old classroom, the grouped tables, the little class library and reading corner, and dollopy paintings all along one wall. There's something different about the smell of this school – warm, and polishy, and dinnery – that made me sad to have left it all behind.

'Jamie's in the sick room,' said Mr Rose. 'I thought it best if he waited for you there. Make sure you get him straight home, won't you?'

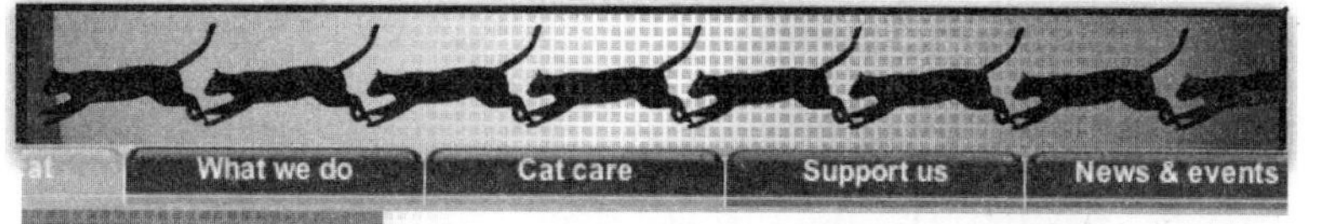

Cats Main Page
About Cats
Pictures of Cats
Myths
Legends
Cat Names
Cat Club

FAQ
Cat Forums

This myth is from Siam, which is now Thailand. They have a cat called the Korat, which is blue grey. Its grey colour is like a rain cloud, and farmers took the cat on a procession when they needed rain for their crops. The farmers pray to the sky gods, and water is sprinkled on the cat's face, which is supposed to make it rain.

A poet from Thailand made up this poem about the Rain Cloud Cat:

'The hairs are smooth
with roots like clouds,
and tips like silver,
and eyes that shine
like dewdrops on a lotus leaf.'

'OK. I'll just tell Noori and Brody not to wait.' I didn't really see what the fuss was about. Maybe Jamie just didn't feel like talking. More often we got told off for talking when we shouldn't.

Two minutes later, I was in Mrs Curwen's office. She's the school secretary, and must be about as old as Nan. 'Hello, Josh! How nice to see you!' she said from behind her desk, all smiles. 'Gosh, you're getting tall! Jamie's the spitting image of you, when you were here.'

Everyone says we're alike, Jamie and me. He's a smaller version of me. We've got the same thick brown hair ('like a thatched roof,' Mum says) and the same greeny-blue eyes as Dad's. We've got some of the same expressions, according to Nan, but of course I can't see what my own face does, so can only go by Jamie's. When he started school, none of the teachers had any trouble knowing who he was – they'd say, 'Oh, you must be Josh's brother!' Still, sometimes, Mr Rose calls him Josh by mistake. That always makes Jamie furious.

'How's things at big school?' Mrs Curwen asked.

'It's OK,' I told her. I was feeling a bit homesick for *this* school, to tell the truth.

She got up and pushed back the curtain to a screened-off area at one side of the office. 'Josh is here, Jamie,' she called. 'You'll be going home in a minute.'

Jamie was huddled up on the bed in there, and Arran was sitting on the edge. He's OK, Arran, and a good little striker. He's Jamie's best friend.

'Jamie? How you feeling?' Mrs Curwen gave his shoulder a nudge.

'All right, Jame?' I said, in a jokey way. 'Thought you'd get out of lessons, did you? Good one!'

Jamie didn't say anything – just looked at me, then hid his face under a curled arm.

'Don't feel like talking today, is that it? Cat got your tongue?' said Mrs Curwen. 'That's what we used to say when I was a girl. Funny old saying, when you think about it.'

'Don't you feel well?' I tried.

No answer.

'Lost your voice? Can't you talk?'

A shrug.

'Has something happened?'

Nothing.

Mrs Curwen looked at Arran. 'You haven't had an argument, you two?'

'No!' Arran shook his head vigorously.

'Did something upset him in the playground? Someone push him, or hurt him, anything like that?'

'I don't know what's wrong!' Arran told her. 'Not a single word since we got to school! I showed him my new calculator and my new coloured pencils and he wasn't even interested.'

'What about this morning, walking in? Did he talk then?' I asked him. We were all talking about Jamie as if he wasn't there. His arm was bent over his face and I couldn't tell whether he was listening or not.

'At first he did. He started telling me about going to stay with your dad.'

'And then?'

'Well, you were waiting for us at the main road, and remember Troy came up and started yakking? I don't think Jamie said any more after that.'

I didn't get this. 'Why should Troy coming up make

Jamie stop talking? What did Troy *say*?'

Arran frowned. 'Can't remember, really. Nothing much. He just sort of witters on and on. That's why I didn't notice Jamie wasn't talking.'

'I phoned your mum, ten minutes ago,' Mrs Curwen told me. 'And I took his temperature, but it's quite normal, so she thought he'd be all right to walk home.'

I wished Mum was coming to fetch him. I don't like anything to do with illness. Mum could easily have walked here in ten minutes, but I suppose she was too busy with the baby as usual.

'We're going home,' I told Jamie. 'Come on! Get your shoes on.'

Nothing.

'Are you mucking about?' I was starting to get impatient. Did he think he was going to lie here all night? I looked at Mrs Curwen, then at Arran.

Mrs Curwen nudged Jamie to make him get up. 'Come on, then! Rise and shine! Josh'll look after you. I expect you'll be right as ninepence when you've had a good rest.'

At last she got him into his shoes and coat and scarf – pushing his arms into the coat sleeves and tying his shoe-laces, like he was one of the infants. I said goodbye to her and Mr Rose, and we set off for home.

The way Jamie walked, you'd have thought he was a zombie. We trailed along like this till we reached Arran's turning. Arran said, 'Bye, Jamie. Hurry up and get better.' Jamie gave no answer – no sign of having heard, even.

I was thinking of what Mrs Curwen had said: *Cat got your tongue?* I'd heard it before, but never really thought about it. It was a horrible idea – a cat swiping someone's tongue out of their mouth, then playing with it, batting it about like Splodge did with his toy mouse. But of course Jamie still *had* a tongue – he was choosing not to use it, that was all.

There was something quite deliberate about this, I felt sure. He could have talked if he wanted to. He was kidding us there was something wrong with him, for a joke or something.

Anyway, we'd be home in a minute. I could stop being sensible big brother, and hand him over to Mum. She'd know what to do.

The problem was, she didn't.

Soon as we got in, she was all over Jamie. 'How do you feel, darling? Are you hot? Dizzy? Tummy-ache? Headache?'

She got him to open his mouth wide so that she could look at his throat. She made him drink hot Ribena. She felt his forehead, she found the thermometer and took his temperature, she asked him again what the matter was. It was no use. Jennie was more talkative than Jamie was – she said 'a-a-ah!' and 'mm!' and other baby sayings that no-one else understood.

'Can you write it down for me?' Mum tried, after she'd run through everything that might possibly be wrong, from sore feet to earache. 'Can you write down why you can't talk? Josh, could you fetch a pencil and paper?'

I ran upstairs and found a blunt pencil, sharpened it, got some drawing paper and went down. Mum had sat Jamie at the table, ready to write.

'Thanks, Josh,' she said. 'Now then, Jamie. Write it

down for me, there's a good boy.'

Jamie picked up the pencil. He felt the sharp point with his finger. He held it in both hands and rolled it between finger and thumb. I watched him, thinking: he's teasing us, making us wait. At last, he gripped the pencil in his right hand, leaned over the paper and drew, very carefully, O.

Mum leaned forward eagerly, waiting for more, but that was it. O.

'O! What does that mean, O? O or naught?'

Jamie put the pencil down and leaned back in his chair. Mum and I both gazed at him, but he didn't look at either of us – he looked towards the window with that odd blank look I was getting used to.

'What does it mean, Jamie?' I started to guess. 'Zero? Nil – like West Ham on Saturday? A circle? A ring? A hoop? O for Orange? Oxygen? Or for Owl . . . Octopus . . . Ostrich?'

Jamie looked at me, and I could tell that this game had got him interested.

'Orang-utan?' I tried. 'Osprey? Okapi?'

He picked up the pencil and carefully shaded in the centre of the O.

'Can't you tell us what it means?' Mum pleaded. 'Write some more, Jamie! Write words!'

But the pencil was lying on the table, and Jamie was sitting back with his arms folded, like infants do to show they've finished.

So the writing hadn't worked, but now I thought of something that might. What if I could get Jamie to laugh?

He's got this peculiar laugh, Jamie has, that sounds like

The Sphinx in Egypt is the most famous lion statue in the world. It has a human head but a lion's body. It guards the ancient kingdom of the pharaohs. The Greeks had a Sphinx with wings, and she terrified everyone by asking them a riddle. Every time the riddle was answered wrongly, she would eat someone.

The **riddle was**, *'What animal goes on all fours in the morning, walks upright in the day and on three legs in the evening?'*

Eventually a man called Oedipus knew the right answer. **MAN** crawls on all fours as a baby, walks on two feet as a grown-up, then leans on a stick when he's old, so the stick is the third leg.

Now that the riddle had been answered correctly, the Sphinx had to kill herself. From this story comes the idea that Sphinxes are very wise.

hiccups. *Hic-hic-hic-a-hic-a-hic-a-hic-a-hicca-a-hic,* he goes. Quite often it *gives* him hiccups. It's the sort of laugh you can't listen to without laughing yourself.

'Mum! I've got an idea,' I whispered.

We retreated to the sink, and Mum switched the kettle on. Its whishing noise covered up what we said – not that Jamie was taking much interest, anyway.

'You know that old Mr Bean video of Mike's?' I said. 'The one where Mr Bean pretends to be a hairdresser and starts cutting people's hair? Jamie loves that. It'll make him laugh. And once he laughs, he might talk.'

'Oh, Josh! That's a clever idea.' Mum's face lost its anxious look. 'Why didn't *I* think of it? You find the tape – I'll bring Jennie in, and we'll all watch it.'

I went back to Jamie. 'Come on, Jamie! We're going to watch Mr Bean!' I found myself doing the thing I'd noticed other people doing – speaking to him very loudly and clearly, as if he was deaf. As if he was an idiot.

Jamie didn't smile, but quite eagerly he got down from the table and into the lounge, where he sat on the sofa. I found Mr Bean, stacked with all the things Mike records and then never gets round to watching. Mum and I settled down to watch – Mum next to Jamie, Jennie lying on her back on her cushioned mat, me sharing the bean bag with Splodge. Splodge thought the bean bag was his, so he gave a little *yah* of protest as I pushed him gently aside. Jamie looked round, startled.

'It's all right, I'm not hurting him!' I brushed white cat-hairs off my sweatshirt. 'I want to share, that's all.'

This Bean tape of Mike's was pretty ancient, but still good. It doesn't spoil it at all, knowing what happens next. Mr Bean's waiting in the barber's when a boy comes in with his mum. The mum mistakes Mr Bean for the hairdresser, so she tells him to cut the boy's hair while she goes somewhere else to find her purse. Mr Bean can't resist having a go. He gets out the clippers and shaves a great thick parting down the middle of the boy's head, making him look a complete prat.

I laughed loudly. So did Mum. The boy looks at himself in the mirror, and instead of going ballistic like you'd expect, he decides he likes it. Then the mum comes back in, and Mr Bean plonks the boy's cap back on before she can see the new haircut. She pays him, and even gives him a tip!

By now, Mum and I were putting on a real laughing performance. It's a lot harder than you'd think. We chuckled and giggled, we rocked with laughter. We collapsed in our seats, limp with laughing. We looked at each other and at Jamie to share every joke. All the time, I took quick little looks at him out of the corner of my eye, and I saw Mum doing the same. He was watching the screen, all right. Once or twice he gave half a smile. But he didn't laugh out loud, not once. Not a single *hic*. It hadn't worked, but just in case, I carried on watching the next episode. Mum sighed, and went out to the kitchen to start getting tea ready.

'Come on, Jamie,' I told him, getting fed up with this. 'It's a game, isn't it? I know you can talk if you want to.'

He looked back at me, and just for a second his mouth quivered as if he was going to speak. Then I saw the determination come back into his face and he gazed at me steadily.

He wasn't mucking about. He was asking me for help.

STRANGER

Jamie was asleep, but I'd never been wider awake.

I couldn't settle. I was in my own bed, in my own room, same as usual. But Jamie wasn't the same as usual, and it felt all wrong.

For as long as I can remember, we've shared a bedroom. I'm used to his snuffles and half-asleep moans, and his annoying way of mumbling when he's reading in bed – not so that I can understand what he's reading, just odd words, that stop me concentrating on *my* book or magazine. And he complains that I snore – yeah, I believe that! – and keep him awake, fidgeting and kicking at my duvet during the night and making my mattress creak.

Now, I'd have *liked* it if he'd complained or read his book aloud. I'd have been really pleased.

It had been an odd kind of evening. In some ways, Jamie was just the same as usual. He ate up all his tea – fish-fingers and mashed potato and peas – and even had an extra helping of ice-cream. Mum had chosen his favourite things, hoping to get some spark of interest out of him. He was keen on eating, all right, but that didn't mean he had anything to say about it.

After tea, Mike got out his pack of cards – we'd all got into card-playing, over Christmas. We started with Sevens, because Jamie likes that best. Then Mike taught us a new game, and Jamie beat us both first go. He smirked, but didn't say a word. Mum made his milk drink and took him up to bed, and spent a while settling him down and reading to him and checking on Jennie. All just the same as any other day.

'Finished your homework, Josh?' Mum said when she came down. I hadn't given it a thought. I took out my book and pens, and sprawled on the front-room floor while Mum and Mike cleared up in the kitchen. They had the radio on and they must have thought I couldn't hear, but I could – Mum's voice was worried, Mike's low and ordinary.

'Wait till tomorrow,' Mike was saying. 'He'll be back to normal, I bet.'

'But what if he isn't?' said Mum. 'What if there's something seriously wrong with him? Like – his vocal chords are paralysed, or something?'

'If he's still not talking, then take him to the doctor,' Mike told her. 'We've agreed that. But I think he's *choosing* not to talk. I don't think there's anything stopping him.'

Mum wasn't having that. 'How can you possibly tell?'

'He's doing it to get attention,' Mike said.

He'd done that all right, I thought, colouring in my picture of a Roman centurion. He'd had *everyone's* attention, all afternoon and all evening.

'Oh, surely not!' went Mum's voice. 'If it were just for

a half an hour or so – but for a child of eight, to say nothing all day long – he'd never be able to keep it up! Not if there wasn't some other reason.'

The next bit was drowned out by the clatter of knives and forks, but then Mike said, 'Kids react in funny ways to having a new baby in the family.'

'Yes, I know! But we've been so careful to make sure Jamie understands – and Josh. We've read the books, we've thought about it, we've done everything we could . . . but none of the books said anything about *this*. Do you think that's what it is? He feels pushed aside by Jennie?'

'Could be.' Mike's voice was muffled, as if his head was in the saucepan cupboard.

'I'll go up and read him an extra bedtime story,' Mum said, 'if he's still awake. And give him another cuddle.'

'OK. I'll get the coffee on. Cappuccino, mocha, espresso, double espresso or latte?'

'Instant, thanks,' Mum said.

I decided to try saying nothing, to see what it felt like. I clamped my mouth shut in case any words got out by accident. I didn't say a word when Mum came down from seeing Jamie, or when Mike came in with the coffee. I concentrated on drawing round my centurion in fine black pen. He'd turned out quite well. I'd done the plumes of his helmet in bright red, and his breastplate in silver, with my felt pens.

'Any luck?' Mike asked Mum.

She shook her head miserably. 'He was already asleep. Well, at least he's *sleeping*. But this is all my fault – it must be!'

'Oh, Liz, come here!' Mike gave her a big hug and a

sloppy kiss, while I made a *yuk* face and bent over my centurion. 'Don't be silly, love! Of course it's not your fault!'

'If only I knew what was going on in his head.' Mum sank wearily on to the sofa.

'He'll be all right tomorrow, you see if he isn't.' Mike had brought in the coffee, and the Belgian chocolates Nan had given us at Christmas. Mum said, 'So much for my New Year diet,' but took one anyway.

'New Year diet! What nonsense. You're feeding Jennie, you need to look after yourself.'

'I need to look after *Jamie*,' Mum said wretchedly.

'You *do* look after him. We both do. And so does Josh. Us Bowmen – sorry, Bowpersons – we look after each other. That's what we're *for.*' Mike passed me the chocolates, and bent down to look over my shoulder. 'Hey! That looks stupendous. You doing a project on the Romans, then?'

'Yes,' I told him. 'He's a centurion. You can tell because he wears his sword on his left side, not his right, and his armour's silver. The ordinary soldiers are called legionaries. See, he's got this special spear, called a pilum – that's for throwing. The sword is for stabbing. His leg-things are called greaves, they protect his legs. And his special sandals are called caligae. This shield's called a scutum. The soldiers had to stay in the army for twenty-five years.'

'Right, Josh. Thanks,' Mike said, looking a bit dazed. 'If I've got any questions, I'll know who to ask.'

I'd completely forgotten about trying not to talk. The words had come straight out of my mouth, as if Mike had pressed a button. It was hard to stay silent at home, never mind at school, with everyone chatting and asking questions. The only way I'd manage to stay quiet all day would be if I gagged myself.

And now here I was, lying in the dark next to my silent brother.

I was thinking: what if Jamie's not there? What if that body in the next bed isn't Jamie at all? What if he's gone – gone for ever?

Little J. Little Josh. Like a little version of me.

Are you there, Jamie? Anyone at home?

Where's my Jamie, the Jamie I'm used to? He's an irritating little pest at times, but he's good fun.

Not much fun as a silent lump, though.

What's got into him?

I thought again about that big O, the only explanation he'd given. Well, clue, at least. He wasn't doing any explaining.

O, I puzzled, O. What could it mean?

A doughnut, a rubber ring, a hula hoop, a football, a plate, a pizza, the Roman Colosseum?

A mouth. An open mouth, with nothing coming out of it.

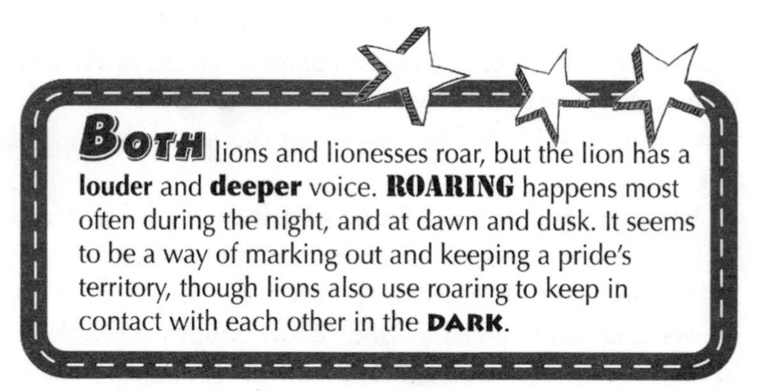

But in the middle of the night, Jamie shouted out. His loud yell of fright grabbed me out of sleep and made my heart pound.

I groped for the light switch and blinked in the sudden brightness.

'Jamie? Hey, what's up?'

Jamie looked at me, his eyes big and startled. There was no way he was going to tell me. He half sat up, leaning against his pillow, clutching the duvet to his chin.

'Wait there!' I said. 'I'll fetch Mum.'

She was already on her way, stumbling across the landing and pulling her dressing-gown round her, with Mike behind, bleary-eyed.

'Was that Jamie?'

'Yes! He shouted – really shouted!'

We all gathered round. In that second when he'd gazed at me, I'd seen Jamie looking out – the Jamie I know. Now his shut-in look had taken over. He sat plucking at the edge of the duvet with his finger and thumb. A tuft of hair curled on top of his head, like Tintin's.

'Hey, Jamie, you gave me a fright!' I said, trying to be normal and friendly.

Mum sat on the bed and smoothed his hair down with her fingers. 'What was it, love? What did you dream?'

Nothing. Jamie gave no sign of having heard. Mum and Mike tried hard. They coaxed him, they fetched a pen and paper, Mike went down and made hot chocolate. Jamie wouldn't respond at all – not even with a nod or a shake of his head.

Eventually, Mum said, 'Mike, could you stay here? I'm taking Jamie to sleep in our bed. I want to be with him if he has another bad dream.'

Obediently, Jamie got out of bed, and Mike got in, yawning. I heard Mum talking and talking to Jamie as she led him across the landing to the big bedroom. Next thing, I bet myself, Jennie would wake up and need feeding.

'You all right, Josh?' Mike was a big man for Jamie's narrow bed, and the mattress creaked as he settled himself. 'Must have made you jump.'

'Yeh, it did.'

'Turn the light out, then, there's a good chap. You've got school tomorrow, and it's another broken night.'

At least, I thought, there couldn't be much wrong with Jamie's vocal chords. Then, across the landing, I heard Jennie starting to cry. Nothing wrong with hers, either.

10
FLOSS

Jamie stayed at home next morning. As early as she could, Mum phoned for an appointment with Dr Awan. When I left for school, Jamie was sitting at the table eating porridge. He gave me a smug look that said, clearly as anything, *You're going to school and I'm not.* I stared back. That was a Jamie look, and it meant Jamie was definitely in there.

First lesson was Drama. For a warm-up, we had to work in pairs and pretend one of us was the mirror reflection of the other. Noori, Brody and I stood together, because some teachers let you stay in a three even when they've said pairs, but Ms Otandu made us swap around. 'Let's mix up the girls and the boys. Brody, you go with Freya. Noori with Sophie. Josh with Floss.'

Brody made a face at me, and Freya moaned, 'Oh, do I *have* to?' She did that thing girls do, rolling her eyes and huffing air at her fringe. She and Brody moved together but stood apart. Floss bounced over to me, smiling.

Floss was new. She'd only started at Langtree two

weeks before we broke up for Christmas. Not only was she new at *our* school, she'd never been to *any* school before. Her parents had been teaching her at home, but now she'd decided for herself that she ought to try school out, and see how she liked it. Mrs Sharman, our form tutor, told us all this before Floss came. Course, everyone had a lot to say about that.

'Never been to school before? Can she read and write?'

'What, you mean we don't *have* to come to school? Why am I here, then?'

'She *wants* to? What, she thinks she's missing something?'

'So if she doesn't like it, she can just clear off back home? Can we all do that if we want?'

'Parents can choose to educate their children at home,' Mrs Sharman explained. 'They have to do it properly, though, covering all the different subjects. They even get inspected, the way schools are. It's not an easy option,' she told us. 'No sitting round watching TV all day – I bet that's what you're imagining, Toby.'

'First time in a school? She hasn't got a flea's chance,' Toby said, when we left our form room for Maths.

Cats are half tame and half wild. It suits them to get used to people and houses, but they're wild as well, with a wild animal's instincts.

I could have told him that the flea is one of the most adaptable creatures around, being a parasite that can jump from one carrier to another, but of course that wasn't what he meant, and I didn't think it was worth sounding like a prize boffin. He must have been imagining, like I was, this quiet, shy thing with pigtails, gazing around in astonishment, getting lost between lessons, being pushed and shoved and teased.

Floss, though, wasn't quiet and shy. Not loud, either. She was just herself. What I mean is, she didn't put on any kind of act. She just seemed to say, 'Well, here I am, folks. This is me.' She was tall and skinny with very blonde hair, and a tanned face even in the middle of winter, and an accent that I thought at first was American, but it turned out to be South African. *Sarth Effrican,* the way Toby and Bex took the mick.

It was her confidence that got those two, and the way she was a bit different, but didn't *mind* being different. One of the things that made her stand out, apart from her height and her accent, was that she didn't immediately pal up with one or two other girls, and stick with them. She'd talk to anyone, girls or boys – just wander over to a conversation or a game, and butt straight in. She didn't know what you do and what you don't do.

That's why Toby set her up with Rick.

Mr O'Shea's the Deputy Head. He's one of the oldest teachers, and the strictest, and always wears a suit. He doesn't have to tell you he means business. He teaches Maths, and although he didn't take our class he'd stood in once when Mr Phillips was away on a course. No one messes about in Mr O'Shea's class, ever. Even Bex, who's got an instinct for winding up teachers, behaves like

Goody-Two-Shoes when Mr O'Shea's around.

It was Noori who nicknamed him Rick – Noori's clever like that. (Rick O'Shea – ricochet – *har har!*) So that's what we all call him now. Not to his face, obviously. You'd have to be a bit kamikaze to do that.

About Floss's third day, Toby came into our form room and handed her a small brown envelope. 'From Mr O'Shea,' he told her. 'Just passed him on my way in. He said to give you this.'

Floss took the note and read it. 'What's all that about?'

Toby looked innocent. 'No idea.'

Later, he told Brody what he'd done – printed out a little note on his computer. It said, 'I need to speak to you about your timetable. Please come to my office at morning break. Ask for Rick.' And he'd signed it with an unreadable signature.

Not surprisingly, Floss does what it says and turns up at his office, in the Admin Area, with her timetable in her hand. 'Hi! I guess you must be Rick,' she says to Mr O'Shea, when he opens his door. He peers at her over the top of his glasses, but he's not stupid, and he knows about Floss being new. 'Round these parts, they tend to call me Mr O'Shea,' he goes. 'It's Florence Darrow, isn't it?'

'Floss, actually,' says Floss, and Rick goes, 'Well, Floss Actually, what can I do for you?' So she says, 'Well, you sent for me,' and he's baffled till she shows him the note. 'I think someone's having a joke at your expense, my dear,' he says. 'Or maybe at mine.'

I got this from Noori, because he saw Toby and Bex setting off behind Floss to hide by the photocopier. Noori had a form about Science Team to hand in to the secretary, so he tagged along behind.

The thing was, when Floss came back to the class for French, she didn't say a single word to Toby about setting her up. All that came out of it was Toby started calling out 'Florence! Flo!' whenever he saw her. She got her own back by calling him Toby Jug. As he had big ears that stuck out like handles, that was soon a class joke, and Floss got a bit of respect.

So, anyway – there we were in Drama, doing this mirror-miming. Floss was good to work with, because she took it seriously and put in all these weird moves, doing a slow glide, then surprising me with a sudden twist or jerk. All the time she had this perfectly serious look on her face that gave nothing away. When it was my turn to lead, she gazed straight at me the whole time, and followed my moves only a nano-second behind. She was good. After that, when we had to make up an improvisation about a misunderstanding, she had smart ideas for that, too.

The problem with Floss was she didn't know the rules. I don't mean the rules about putting your litter in the bin and not running in corridors. I mean the unwritten rules. For example, everyone knows that if you're a boy, you don't go and sit next to a girl, and if you're a girl, you don't willingly sit next to a boy – unless you're Toby and Bex, that is. Some of the teachers mix us up, but left to ourselves you'd think we were two separate species. Boys, when girls are around, are like iron filings repelled from the wrong end of a magnet.

Next lesson after Drama, the heating had broken in the mobile where we usually have French, so we were moved to one of the Maths rooms. Noori and Brody sat together with me in the row in front, and a spare place next to me. That was OK, I liked having room to spread out, and I could turn round to them when we had the conversation practice. Mr Dawkins checked our names and was handing out books when Floss strolled in, smiling vaguely.

'Yes?' said Mr Dawkins, a bit snappish. He was already irritated, because of the room change.

Floss looked at him, and said, 'I'm here for French.'

'What I *meant,*' Mr D explained patiently, 'is that when you're late for a lesson, you're expected to offer an apology.'

'Oh. Well, see, I got talking to Wilbur, and then I didn't know what room to come to.'

There's only one Wilbur at school, and that's Wilbur Evans, the Site Manager. Two weeks in school, and Floss had made friends with him. She chatted to everyone.

'*Mr Evans* has work to do, and so do you,' said Mr Dawkins. 'Take a seat.'

I knew what would happen then. Floss gazed around the room looking for a place, saw me, and came straight over. We had to spend the rest of the lesson *parlez-vous*ing about shopping in the *boulangerie* and the *supermarché.* Floss knew French quite well, only she spoke it with a South African accent.

Of course, that was it. Two lessons in one day! According to Bex, that made us an *item.* 'Josh and Floss!' she chanted. Others joined in, and by lunchtime it had become *JoshnFloss.* 'Hey, there's JoshnFloss! How *sweet*!'

Noori nudged me. 'Bowandarrow? Josh Bowman and Florence Darrow?'

He'd said it quietly, but Brody started going, 'Bowandarrow! Bowandarrow!' and jigged round pretending to aim arrows at me.

'Thanks a lot.' I glared at both of them.

Course, Bex overheard. From then on it was *JoshnFloss! Bowandarrow!* even when Floss and I weren't within twenty metres of each other, which I made sure was most of the time.

11
SATSUMA JUGGLING

A phone message was brought to our classroom at afternoon registration. It said: *Joshua Bowman 7SS. Your mum phoned. Jamie's at school this afternoon so she'll meet you 3.40 outside the primary school.*

I thought this meant the doctor had given Jamie a pill or an injection and changed him back into Normal Speaking Boy. I was wrong.

We had PE last thing, so I was a bit later at St Luke's than usual. Jamie was already by the gate with Mum, holding on to the buggy, wearing his no-one-at-home face. There was a chill in the air that felt almost dangerous, making me shiver at the thought of night's cold grip and the darkness to come. Jennie, in the buggy, was zipped up in one of those all-in-one padded suits, with a hood, so all you could see was the pale little circle of her face.

'Hi, Mum. Hi, Jamie.' Then I remembered to say, 'Hi, Jennie,' as well. I waited till we were walking along the pavement before whispering to Mum, 'What did the doctor say, then?'

'We're going back in two days.' Mum darted an anxious look at Jamie, who trundled along beside us, his head round and neat in a Chelsea knitted hat. 'Dr Awan thought he might as well be at school, as he's otherwise behaving normally – it's more stimulating for him than sitting at home. And he might just start to speak again, but Mr Rose says he's not made a sound since I brought him at lunchtime.'

'Didn't the doctor give him any pills or medicine or anything?'

'It's not as simple as that, Josh.'

I kicked at a twig. 'So it was useless, then, taking him?' If doctors couldn't do anything, who could?

'Oh no, it wasn't useless. She looked at his ears and throat and eyes, and at least she doesn't think there's anything physically wrong.' Mum lowered her voice. 'If there's no change when we go back, she'll refer us to a child psychologist. A specialist. Someone who's used to this sort of thing, and can give us some help.'

'This sort of thing?'

'Yes. It's unusual, but it does happen to other children. So, Jamie!' Mum said, suddenly putting on a louder, cheerful voice. 'Mr Rose told me you're having a visit tomorrow from some mime artists – that'll be fun, won't it? I wish I could come!'

And she chattered away to Jamie, while it was my turn to fall silent. My brain kept circling round one word. *Psychologist.*

Normal people don't go to psychologists. I mean, it's not like the dentist or the optician. 'I've got the psychologist this afternoon – just a check-up!'

No. Psychologists are for mad people, aren't they?

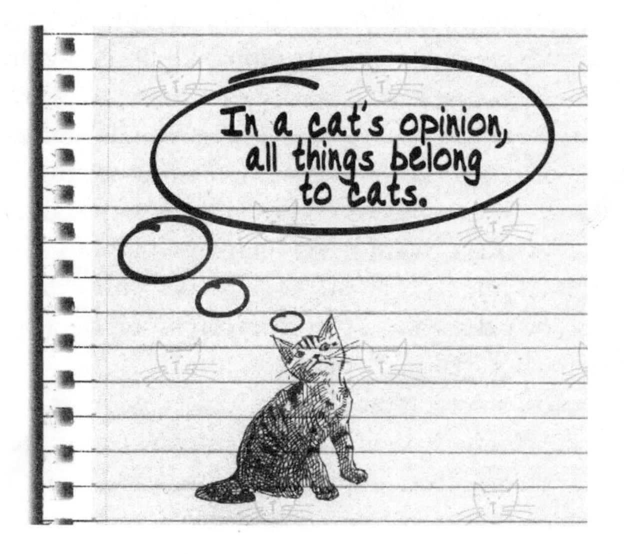

Soon as we got in, I Googled *psychologist*. Once I'd learned how to spell it right, a whole list came up. It was well confusing. From this list, I found out there are clinical psychologists, forensic psychologists, counselling psychologists, health psychologists and even industrial psychologists. There were lots of long articles with words I couldn't understand. But nothing that said what to do if your brother suddenly stopped talking.

Then at last I found something that explained what psychology *is*, and it seemed quite simple after all:

> WHAT IS PSYCHOLOGY?
> Psychology is a science-based profession. It is the study of people: how they think, how they act, react and interact. It is concerned with all aspects of behaviour and the thoughts, feelings and motivation underlying such behaviour.

Well, I thought, is that all? Just study? Just behaviour? No electrodes, brain scans or impossible tests? I could do that! I'm good at studying, and after all, no stranger could study Jamie better than I could. I've known him all his life. I share a bedroom with him. I know all his habits: how funny he can be, how annoying, what he likes and doesn't like to eat, what makes him laugh.

It seemed ages since I'd heard that funny hiccuppy laugh of his. I missed it. Mr Bean hadn't managed to make him laugh, but maybe *I* could.

So I tried. I went down to the front room, and found him sitting on the sofa looking at the television, though it wasn't even switched on. I'd give him something better than TV to look at. I told jokes, I did silly walks. I tried to walk on my hands, and nose-dived to the carpet.

Jamie stared, like I'd gone mental. Like *I'd* gone mental.

'Oh, come on!' I told him. 'You could *try* joining in!'

Running out of things to do, I picked up three satsumas from the fruit bowl and started trying to juggle. It was harder than I thought. The satsumas were bashed and dented from rolling all over the floor by the time Mike came in and saw what I was doing.

'No, Josh, no,' he went, and I thought he was telling me off for wasting satsumas. But instead he collected them up, and said, 'You don't pass from one hand to the other. Juggling's all about *throwing*.' And off he went.

How was I to know Mike was a secret juggler? He was good, even when I threw in an apple. Then he nodded for me to chuck in a banana as well, and they all went whirling round like an airborne fruit salad.

Course, Jamie couldn't sit watching this without

wanting a go himself. He wasn't even as good as me, which wasn't saying much, and soon Splodge got fed up with having to dodge flying fruit every few seconds and went to hide behind the TV cabinet, but the important thing was that Jamie was looking like Jamie. He was even doing a few *hic-hic-hics,* not exactly laughing, but sort of revving-up towards laughing, with all the effort of concentrating. We did this until Mum came down and asked Jamie if he wanted to help bath Jennie and put her to bed. It turned out that Mum didn't know Mike could juggle either, so he had to do more demonstrating, and then she had a go. When they were all tired of juggling except me – if Mike could keep five things in the air, surely I could manage *three* – Jamie went upstairs with her quite willingly to see to Jennie.

I knew what she was doing, with all this *help me with Jennie* stuff. It was a way of making Jamie feel important and responsible. I helped out too, but I'm older and don't need such special treatment. Anyway, I was already interested. To me, Jennie was a baby animal, so she was nearly as fascinating as a baby gorilla would be, or a tiger cub. The thing is about animals, from the moment they're born, or even before that, they've got all this stuff programmed into them. What to do. What to eat. What to be frightened of.

Compared with most baby animals, humans are quite backward. A foal can run with the herd within hours of being born, and a duckling or a cygnet knows how to swim. But all a baby like Jennie can do is lie in her pram, and drink milk, and wee and poo, and cry and sleep. She's pretty helpless really. A baby orang-utan or a chimpanzee would have been a lot more fun, or my first choice, a mountain gorilla (*gorilla gorilla beringei*), but since I wasn't likely to get any of those, I'd make do with Jennie. I liked seeing how things changed from week to week. For instance, when she was first born she didn't even know how to look at people's faces. Now she could do that. And if you put your finger near her hand, she'd curl her tiny fingers round it. Actually, I know a lot about babies, from reading Mum's books. Like, just before ours was born, I thought Mum ought to know that Jennie had hair about two inches long and her fingernails already needed clipping. Mum said the baby would have to wait till she was out in the world before she got her first manicure, but I could tell she was impressed.

Jamie was a bit young to be interested. Some of the book was a bit yukky even for me, and I can take most things. I skipped all the ikky stuff about how babies get made – anyway, we'd got past that stage before Mike bought the book – and stuck to the facts about foetal development.

By the time I went to bed, I was getting a bit fed up with Jamie, to be honest. I was quite sure he only wanted lots of fuss made of him. I nearly told him so. But I remembered that I was studying him, and that meant not interfering. What I wanted to do was catch him out.

12
MASK

Next day, at the end of school, I went across to the juniors as usual, with Brody and Noori, to collect Jamie. Soon as I got to the gate, and all the mums waiting with their buggies, I heard, 'Hey, Josh!' and Jamie's friend Arran ran towards me. He must have been waiting.

'Mr Rose says can you come in?' he panted. 'Jamie's been *talking*!'

'What's that about?' I heard Noori ask Brody.

'Jamie's gone peculiar,' Brody said. 'They're sending him to a psychiatrist.'

Psychiatrist isn't the same as psychologist, but I couldn't stop now to put Brody right. I ran in with Arran, outpacing him.

'Talking?' I asked, turning to run backwards, so he could catch up. 'What, just like normal?'

'Well, no. It's a bit odd, to say the least. He's being a cat!'

'A *cat*? How?'

'We had these mime people in our class, and we've been

making masks and using them to make up plays . . .'

But now we were at Mr Rose's door, and Mr Rose was waiting there.

'Thanks, Arran,' he said, and nodded for Arran to go into the classroom. To me, he said, 'I've just asked Mrs Curwen to phone your mum – I think she'll want to come straight away. It's a bit odd, Josh. We've been making masks, and Jamie made a cat's face. And as soon as he put the mask on, he started to talk. Only not as himself. As the cat.'

'What did he say?'

Mr Rose frowned. 'He said things like *I can see you*,' he went, in this strange drawly way. '*I know what you're thinking*.'

Jamie's sign of the Zodiac is Leo because his birthday is on August 3rd. Leo is the king of animals and is noble, proud and generous. Leo people are proud and generous too. They like to be the centre of attention, and they often act dramatically.

Mum's Leo as well, but she's a quiet and undramatic person, so the Zodiac signs don't fit everyone.

'He said that? In that funny voice?'

'Yes. Come in and see if he's still doing it. Maybe he'll talk to you.'

I didn't like what I saw. While Mr Rose had been out of the room, a crowd of children had gathered round Jamie. Most of them wore masks – blodgy clown faces or cartoon characters. Jamie, in a painted cat's mask, was sitting at his desk, with his hands curled in front of him like paws. He's quite good at drawing and painting, better than me. His mask was of a bold yellow cat, a lion, with sprouting whiskers and carefully-shaped eye-slits. I couldn't see Jamie's eyes behind, but the slitty shapes gave the face a cat's fierce stare.

His gaze was fixed on a little girl with hair in lots of little plaits that sprouted from her head like antennae. '*You think you can hide,*' he told her, in the slow, yowly voice Mr Rose had tried to copy, '*but I'll know where you've gone. I can come and find you whenever I want.*'

For a few seconds the girl seemed hypnotised, then she ducked her face down and squirmed away, and some of the others squealed. A boy in an alien mask pushed forward, wanting attention. 'Do it to me, Jamie!'

Jamie was a freak show. A circus act. I wanted to shout at the children, tell them to leave him alone. I started to swish them away like wasps.

Mr Rose's big voice cut through the squealing and giggling. 'Back to your own tables, everyone! *Now!* I want paintbrushes washed, everything cleared up, and all of you ready for home, in three minutes.'

Now the room was full of the sounds of scraping chairs and running taps and chatter. In the middle of it all, I sat next to Jamie. He seemed even more silent than before, with the cat mask between him and me. On the table was a sheet of paper with lines of writing on it, set out in play script.

'That's what we've been doing,' said Arran, seeing me looking. 'We made up plays for our characters.'

'So who were you?'

His mask was face-down on the table, so all I could see was the elastic that would hold it in place. When he held it up to show me, I didn't get it. Unlike the other children, who'd painted monsters or clowns, Arran had made an ordinary face. Smiley mouth, brown hair flopping in a fringe, round red cheeks.

'Who's that?' I asked.

'Can't you tell?' He sounded disappointed. 'It's meant to be *him*!'

'You've made a mask of Jamie?'

He pulled a face. 'Well, tried. It's not very good.'

'Put it on!'

Arran put the mask over his face, then pulled Jamie's Chelsea hat over his head. He tugged it down over the top of the mask, making the cardboard crease and buckle. So now we had Jamie as a cat, Arran as Jamie.

'Who are you?' I asked Jamie, all casual.

Slowly he turned his head to me. 'Leo. I'm Leo.'

Leo for Lion, *panthera leo,* but also it's his middle name. He was christened Jamie Leo Bryce, now Jamie Leo Bowman. Mum and Dad thought of that because Leo's his Zodiac sign. Pity they didn't think of it when I was born – instead of Joshua Paul, I'd be Joshua Scorpio.

'Is Jamie in there?' I asked, not sure whether it was the right thing to say. I didn't know how to get through to him, this cat-stranger. But he was talking, for the first time in two days! I wanted to know everything at once – *what's happened to you? What made you lose your voice? Why have you started talking now, and in this cat voice – what's that about?*

Jamie shook his head vigorously, pointing at Arran. '*That's* Jamie. Duh! I'm Leo.'

'Want to read me your play?' I said. I didn't think it could be very long, and we'd have a couple of minutes. Mr Rose saw what I was doing, and left us to it while he chivvied the rest of the class to finish at the sink and put books and pencils away in trays.

This is what Jamie and Arran read out:

Arran-as-Jamie: *What are you staring at?*
Jamie-as-Leo: *You. Because you have to follow me. I make you.*
Arran-as-Jamie: *How do you make me?*
Jamie-as-Leo: *Because you're mine. I told you.*
Arran-as-Jamie: *How did you tell me?*
Jamie-as-Leo: *When I looked at you.*
Arran-as-Jamie: *When did you look at me?*
Jamie-as-Leo: *When I was a lion.*
Arran-as-Jamie: *But you* are *a lion.*
Jamie-as-Leo: *I know. I mean when you came to see me. When you looked in my cage and I looked back at you.*
Arran-as-Jamie: *Yes?*
Jamie-as-Leo: *I looked at you and I said –*
Pause.
Arran-as-Jamie: *Yes? What did you say?*
Jamie-as-Leo: *I looked at you and I said –*
Pause.

I sat forward, eager. 'What? What did you say?' I had to make myself speak calmly, when inside I was fizzing with excitement.

Nothing. I'd pushed too far – spoiled it. Jamie had gone silent again. He turned to stare at me from behind his mask. And his stare seemed to say, *But you know! Or if you don't know, you ought to.*

I remembered him telling me on the Ridgeway walk that the lion had spoken to him, but he couldn't remember what. I thought he was just inventing it – well, and of course he *was*.

'That's as far as we've got,' Arran told me. 'We're supposed to finish tomorrow.'

He took off his Jamie mask and walked across to put it carefully in his tray. I folded the play-script and put it in my pocket. I wanted to read it again later, and copy it out to keep. If Jamie had caught the Lion thing – only turbo-charged – and now he was a head case, it must be down to me to sort it out, mustn't it? He must have got it from me. I'm always wondering what cats think and dream and fear. I'm always wishing I could get inside Splodge's head to see what it feels like in there – to see what he thinks about *me*, and about other humans. But I'd never thought I actually *was* a cat or a lion.

All the children were standing behind their desks now, ready to be dismissed. Jamie stood, too, still wearing the lion face.

'You can't go home wearing that, Jamie – you'll scare the infants!' Mr Rose joked. 'Take it off

and put it in your tray. Well done – you and Arran worked really well together.'

But Jamie wouldn't be parted from his mask. He insisted on wearing it all the way home.

13
LEO

All evening, we had to pretend he was Leo.

'D'you want the TV on, Leo?'

'Milk-shake or orange-juice, Leo?'

'Shall I read you a story, Leo?'

Some of the questions Jamie answered in his Leo voice. To others, he only gave a nod or a shake of his head. As Leo he was stern and kingly.

Mum went into the kitchen to get the tea, leaving me and Jamie to keep an eye on Jennie in the lounge. Course, Mum was delighted that Jamie had started talking, but she didn't know the half of it. I followed her to the kitchen.

'Mum? You know this Leo thing?' I said. 'At school? It was weird. Jamie and Arran were making up a play together – Jamie was Leo, and Arran was Jamie.'

Mum unplugged the kettle and took it to the sink. 'A play? That sounds like fun. And that's when Jamie started to talk?'

I nodded. 'But Mum, you know we went to that wildlife park, with Dad? And saw lions?'

'Mm?'

'Well, in the play, Jamie said the lion told him something. He said that before, too.'

Mum stared at me, then jumped back as tap-water sprayed all over the lid of the kettle and soaked the sleeve of her jumper. 'Oh, *now* look.' She turned off the tap. 'He said *what?*'

'The lion told him something. I was waiting for him to say *what,* but that was as far as they'd got, with the play.'

'Oh, but he was just pretending, surely!' Mum dabbed at her sleeve with a towel.

'Well, course he was!' I humphed. 'I mean, the lion didn't *really* talk! But—' I stood by the draining-board, remembering the lion's steady gaze, and the shudder that had gone through me. No, not really a shudder. I hadn't been frightened, I'd been – hypnotised. I couldn't have moved if I'd wanted to. I was held by that fiercely calm gaze like a hedgehog in car headlights. Perhaps the lion had told me something, too, sent me a message . . . if I could only *understand* . . .

'But what?' Mum prompted.

'Well, look at this.' As soon as we'd got in from school, I'd typed a copy of the play-script Jamie and Arran had written, and printed it out. I took the page out of my jeans pocket and gave it to her. 'Here's what they did. See, Jamie was Leo, and Arran was Jamie – his mask was meant to be Jamie. But it's not finished, Arran said.'

'Arran was Jamie? Whatever made him think of that?'

I shook my head – how would I know? Mum read the script, slowly, her lips shaping the words. Then she went back to the beginning and started again. I didn't like what I'd just done – taking Jamie's script without asking, using it as evidence. Too late, now. Mum had it in her hand.

'Are they going to finish it?' she said at last. 'If only we knew what the lion said! I mean, what he *thought* it said.'

'Tomorrow,' I told her. 'They're doing more on it tomorrow.'

'Can I keep this?'

'If you want.' I'd been going to put it in my Book of Cats, but I could print out another copy.

'I'd like to show it to the – to the doctor,' Mum said.

What she meant was the *psychologist*.

She tucked the paper into the rack where she keeps letters and vouchers and free offers. 'Thanks, Josh. I'm glad you showed me. I wonder if I ought to speak to Mr Rose about this. Jamie needs time to finish this in his own way.'

Suddenly a look of panic came over her face, and she rushed into the lounge. Maybe she'd heard Jennie crying, or starting to cry – she seemed to have developed extra-sensory perception since Jennie had been born. I followed, but Jennie was lying peacefully in her crib, clenching and unclenching her fists the way she did sometimes, and Jamie was curled up on the sofa, still with his Leo mask on, looking at my wildlife magazine. I looked at Mum. Had she thought Jamie might hurt Jennie?

'Tea in ten minutes, boys,' Mum said.

She'd already forgotten that Jamie only answered to *Leo*.

We were eating apple pie when I heard the rumble and clatter of Mike's van on the driveway. He was late, because he'd been trying to finish a job in Cricklewood. I thought Jamie would have to take off his mask to eat – Mum hadn't tried to make him, but had watched to see what he'd do. What he did, he pushed it up for each mouthful, then pulled it back quickly while he chewed and swallowed, hiding himself. He wouldn't look at me or Mum, or join in the conversation.

What if he really had been taken over by something, some spirit of Leo or Lion that had turned him into a different person? What if the eyes behind the mask weren't Jamie's, but the glaring amber eyes of a lion? I tried to concentrate on eating my pie and making things seem normal. This was just stupid. If I got frightened of my own brother, what use would I be?

Mike came in, all dusty and cement-spattered in his

overalls. Instead of giving us all a hug as usual, he stared at Jamie, surprised by the mask. Jamie stared back through the eye-slits. There was an odd stillness about him. A lion waiting to spring, I thought. There really was a stranger at our table. But Mike recovered quickly.

'Wow, Jamie!' he said. 'That's stupendous! Did you make it? You'll scare Splodge – he'll think there's an intruder in the house!'

'He's Leo,' I told Mike. 'You have to call him Leo.'

Mike looked astonished. He always goes upstairs to change out of his work clothes as soon as he's home from work, but today was different.

'Come and sit down,' Mum told him. 'We're having tea – Josh, me and Leo. Say hello to Mike, Leo.'

'I'm Leo. You can't tell me what to do,' said Jamie in his Leo voice.

Very slowly, holding out his hands to the table to steady himself, Mike sat down. 'Hello, Leo,' he said.

Jamie nodded his head sternly.

'Have you come to live with us?' Mike gave a quick glance at Mum to check he was doing it right.

'I might stay for a bit,' Jamie said. 'I live wherever I want. I'm Leo.'

'Well, we're very pleased to have you here,' Mike said. He looked at the plates on the table. 'Have you had something nice to eat? What do you like, I wonder? Pilchards? Minced rabbit?'

'I've eaten, thank you,' Jamie said.

'You mustn't joke with Leo,' I whispered to Mike. 'He's a lion, a proud lion, not an ordinary cat.'

Mike nodded, then continued to Jamie: 'How did you manage to eat your tea with the mask on?'

Jamie showed no sign of having heard. I thought: while he's Leo, it isn't a mask – it's *him*. That's why he won't answer.

'He pushed the mask up to put food in his mouth,' Mum explained. 'And down again while he chewed.'

'I eat what I like,' Jamie said. 'And I like baked beans.' It was almost his normal voice.

'Good, so do I.' Mike darted another look at Mum. 'Have you left me any?' I could see that they both felt the way I had at school – fidgety with excitement, sure that we'd almost got Jamie back.

We hadn't. Only Jamie-as-Leo.

When it was Jamie's bed-time, I went upstairs to fetch my Book of Cats. With difficulty, Mum persuaded him to take off the Leo face. 'You can wear it again tomorrow, if you want.'

Reluctantly, Jamie lifted off the mask and put it on the low table between our two beds.

'Have you cleaned your teeth?'

No answer.

'Would you like a story?'

No answer.

Without the mask, Jamie was shut back into silence.

14
LOO-BRUSH

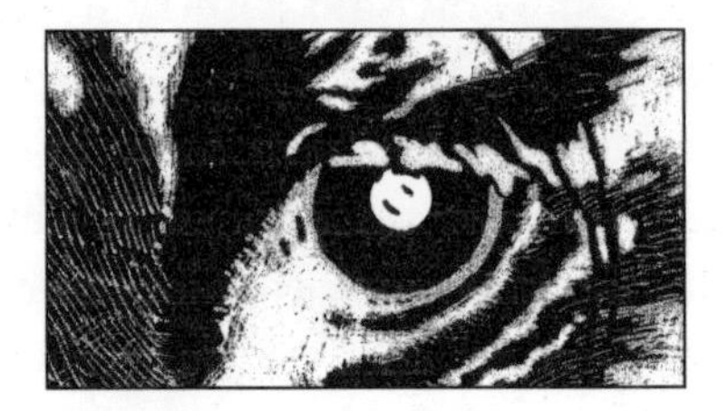

We'd all been so busy with Jamie that I hadn't noticed Splodge wasn't around. Now, I realised I hadn't seen him since we got in from school. Surely he hadn't been outside all this time – soft old Splodge, who spent half his life sleeping on cushions? I looked round for him – the bean bag, the windowsill, the back of the sofa where he got the warmth of the radiator. Next I tried his upstairs places, but still couldn't find him.

When I went back down, Mum and Mike were in the front room, sitting together on the sofa.

'I just don't understand it,' Mum was saying. 'Dr Awan was quite right – there's nothing *stopping* him from talking. It seems to be the mask that made him start to speak. It's so peculiar – like he's hiding behind it!'

'Perhaps he feels safer that way?' Mike suggested.

'But why? Why should he feel unsafe without it? Are you saying he feels unsafe here with us, with his family?'

Mike gave a *search me* shrug. 'I don't know, love, I really don't. I was just trying to think of something that makes sense. Are you taking him back to the doctor's tomorrow?'

'Yes, I will. But I think it's the psychologist we need, not the doctor.'

'Why don't you give Paul a ring? Get him to come over. Maybe Jamie needs his own Dad. Maybe Paul could even go to the doctor's with you. Or the psychologist.'

'Well – yes, maybe I will –'

'Mum,' I broke in, 'where's Splodge? I haven't seen him since I got in from school.'

Mum turned to me, her face pinched up with a new worry. 'No! He hasn't been around, has he?'

'Well, when did you last see him?' I demanded.

'He was definitely here when I gave Jennie her bath, because he sat on the toilet seat watching – you know how he does. But I don't think I've seen him since.'

Mike frowned. 'No. I've not seen him, either.'

'What, you didn't feed him?' I accused Mum.

'No, I forgot, with all this Leo business going on.'

'But he never *lets* us forget! He's never missed a meal in his entire *life*!'

'Then that must mean he wasn't here,' Mum said. 'I'd have tripped over him fifteen times while I was getting tea, otherwise.'

'Why didn't you say? How come you didn't notice?'

'Josh,' Mum said, 'I've got quite enough on my plate, don't you think? Without you pestering me about the cat. Splodge can look after himself.'

I hated it when she spoke to me in that tired, patient voice. I turned away. 'I'm going to look outside.'

'Don't worry! He won't be far away,' Mike said. 'He'll turn up as soon as he's hungry, old Splodge the Podge.'

'But he's *always* hungry. I've got to find him.'

'It's dark, Josh – don't go far. I don't want you wandering about,' Mum fretted.

'I'm only going in the garden. Not on a Polar expedition.'

I was in a mood to be fed up with everyone – with Mum, with Jamie, with Splodge for disappearing, even with Mike, for telling me not to worry, when I *wanted* to worry.

Nothing was the same any more. We couldn't just be normal, not since the baby.

It was all Jennie's fault! It must be. Jennie kept Mum tied to nappies and feeds and bathtimes. Jennie spoiled Mum's sleep, making Mum get up in the middle of the night when she cried. Everything had been fine, before Jennie. Now it was all *baby baby baby,* apart from the times when it was *Jamie Jamie Jamie* – you'd think no one else mattered.

My bad mood had sneaked up on me like a head cold, filling me up with it. I felt spiky and tight and irritable – I hated it, but didn't know how to get rid of it, any more than I could get rid of the sneezes and the runny nose once a cold took grip. I wasn't used to this! Mum was always saying how good-natured I am, how helpful, what a good brother to Jamie and Jennie. Just now I didn't feel like being good or kind or helpful to *any*one. As for Jamie, and all this Leo business – he was just copying me, that's all it was. Cats are mine, and I'm not sharing them. This was a stupid, babyish thing to think, and I knew it. That only made me crosser.

'Put your coat on, Josh, if you're going outside,' Mum called.

'Gloves, too, and don't be more than a few minutes.' That was Mike. 'It must be sub-zero out there.'

'Yeah, yeah,' I muttered. 'Leave me alone, will you?'

I took my coat from its peg and stomped out of the back door, shutting it hard behind me.

Outside was so different from in, on this cold, cold night. We're like cave people, barricading ourselves in with our lights and our fires against the chill and the dark, but it's still out there, bigger than we can imagine. Same as it's always been, always will be. We've got central heating and television and the internet, but we're still living on this little spinning planet in the middle of all that dark, just like the earliest humans did.

Thinking that made me feel tiny and unimportant. But at the same time bigger inside, like being on the edge of understanding something.

It wasn't nine o'clock yet, but it felt like stepping out into the middle of the night. Cold air pressed against my face, bit at my hands, streamed into my ears and round the back of my neck and through my jeans. I stood for a few moments on the patio, my back against the bright square of the kitchen window, letting my eyes adjust.

Gradually, the high garden fence came into focus, a black slab against the sky, and there were street lamps beyond the high trees at the end of our garden, and lit windows in other houses. There was a sprinkling of stars, and a wisp of cloud like a scarf. As I looked, there were more and more and more stars, some bright and gold, others tiny pin-pricks. Course, they don't look as bright as they would without the street lights. What was it like to be Early Man, even earlier than fire, with the only light coming from the stars and the moon? I felt dizzy, as if there was no up or down. I'd lose my balance, and tumble into the hugeness that stretches out for ever.

I moved my feet, to convince myself I was standing firm on the ground. They'd already started to go numb.

'Splodge!' I shouted. 'Splodgey! Splodge, come here!'

I should have brought a torch.

'Please!' I added.

My voice floated away, up and up, towards the stars. There was no one to hear me. I waited for Splodge's chirruping Hello, and his furry warmth against my leg. My eyes strained for the white bits of him – on the fence, among the shrubs. I knew how he came out of the dark – his white splashes like pieces of torn rag, then they suddenly make themselves into a whole purring cat. I walked up the garden path, making myself as tall as I could so that my voice would carry over to Doug's garden next door. Splodge goes over there sometimes.

'Splodge! Splodgey! You've missed your dinner!'

A shiver went down my back. What if cat eyes were watching me in the darkness? What if cat shapes were crouching among the plants?

What was the matter with me? I was only looking for my cat. I looked in every corner of the garden, still calling. No Splodge. I hated the thought of him melting into the dark, hearing me but choosing not to come.

It was so cold that I felt it in my teeth. Mike was right, I needed gloves and a woolly hat as well as my coat. In the morning the pavements would be silvered with frost. If I went back in, Splodge would quite likely sneak in through his cat flap in the next few minutes. And I hadn't *really* looked everywhere indoors. Perhaps he'd found a new hiding-place. With the choice between a centrally-heated house and an icy cold garden, what sensible cat would be outside?

I let myself back in. Mum and Mike were still close together on the sofa, and I saw a tear-trail down Mum's face. I looked away.

'Any luck?' Mike said in the fake-cheerful voice he used when he was trying to pretend nothing was wrong.

'No. No sign of him. I'm going to look upstairs.'

'He shouldn't *be* upstairs,' Mum said, getting agitated all over again. 'Not when Jennie's asleep in her cot. You know that!'

'Yeah, right, have a go at me!' I felt myself going hot. 'Why's it *my* fault?'

Mike looked at me sharply and I thought he was going to tell me off, but he only said, 'Well, he's got to be *some*where.'

I stomped up the stairs.

'Don't wake Jennie,' Mum called after me. 'Or Jamie.'

Jamie was asleep. I looked under both our beds, and pulled back my duvet, even though it was obvious there was no Splodge-hump under it. I looked behind the curtains. Then I went into Mum and Mike's room. Mum leaves a night-light on, one of those things you plug straight into a socket, so that she can check on Jennie without having to switch on the main light or a lamp. I looked into Jennie's cot.

She was lying on her back, with her head turned to one side. Her eyes were closed. I couldn't see now, but I knew that her eyelids were the softest mauvey-white, like the curved inside of a sea-shell. She made a small snuffling sound as she breathed. Her mouth was slightly open, then it made a sort of mumbling movement, and she dribbled a bit.

All my bad temper came foaming up. Like when you drink Coke too quickly and it's all fizzing inside, and you need to burp or sneeze to let some of it out.

'It's all your fault!' I told her. 'Everything was fine, till you came along. I wish you'd go away.'

There, I'd said it! I stood tall over the cot, triumphant. My voice sounded strange – rough and harsh and hissy. For a second I thought it was someone else speaking. The words echoed in my ears.

But it wasn't someone else. It was me, loud and clear.

What was I doing, saying nasty things to a sleeping baby?

I knelt down and leaned into the cot. 'Jennie, I didn't mean it!' I whispered. 'It wasn't me! I don't know why I said it! You didn't hear, did you?'

She stirred and made a tiny whimper, but didn't wake up.

I watched her for a few more moments, hardly breathing. Then I stretched out a finger and touched her hand. Brand-new skin, living and warm, with fingernails, and little bones underneath even though I couldn't feel them, all the same bones I've got in my much bigger hand. Our little miracle, Mike calls her. The way she's made. The way she's got everything in her she needs to be a real grown-up person. His beautiful little package, he calls her. Sometimes he goes all soft and soppy, cooing and muttering and cuddling her and talking all sorts of nonsense. He's like a kid with a new toy, Mum says, only Jennie isn't a toy. The girl she's going to be, the girl we'll get to know, my sister – where did she come from, that person? Where had she been till now?

Although I like facts so much, I also liked this not-understanding. This wondering. I smiled at Jennie, and touched her cheek. I felt how firm it was, how real. She was here now.

It was only when I went down again, and saw Mum and Mike both staring at me, and the almost frightened expression on Mum's face, that a thump of shame and guilt slammed through me and I knew what had happened. They'd heard! Heard what I said to Jennie! Mum's never far from the baby monitor. My horrible words would have been relayed down here five times more loudly than I'd spoken them. Or maybe she'd forgotten to switch it on?

My feet seemed to be superglued to the floor. I couldn't move. Couldn't speak. But I felt my face flaming red, my heart pumping and my ears burning.

Neither of them spoke.

Perhaps they *hadn't* heard? Perhaps the monitor wasn't on after all?

'No luck with Splodger the Dodger?' was all Mike said. 'Did you try the airing cupboard?'

'No!' Glad to get away, I raced back upstairs. The door on the landing was slightly open.

'Splodge? You in there?'

The airing-cupboard is where Splodge hides when there's a thunderstorm, or fireworks, which are even worse. He stays in there for hours. He knows how to pull the door open by hooking it with his front paw, which is quite clever of him. I opened the door and knelt down on the carpet. There he was, crouched into the back corner, behind the tank.

'Come on, you silly old lump! What're you hiding for?'

I tried to pull him out. He shrank back, and I had to reach in with both hands. Eventually I had him in my arms, stiff and resisting.

'What's the matter?' I said into his fur.

I wanted to take him downstairs and give him his dinner, but Splodge didn't want to be carried. While I was awkwardly trying to stand up, he struggled free, scratching my arm hard with the claws of his back feet. Then he rocketed down the stairs. His tail was fluffed out, the way it goes if a dog chases him in the street.

I ran down after him.

'Was that Splodge, or a piebald whirlwind?' Mike was on his feet, looking behind the sofa.

'Come out, scaredy-cat!' I got down on all fours. Splodge was crouching there, between the sofa and the wall.

'Come here, puss-puss-puss!' Mike tried, from the other end.

Splodge was looking one way then the other, quick and scared, with his ears pressed flat back. He looked ugly like that, some terrified wild thing, not my usual silly, softy

Splodge-Face. I could see his tail, fluffed out to three times its usual size.

'Leave him,' said Mum. 'He'll come out when he's ready.'

Mike got to his feet. 'Something's scared him. His tail's gone loo-brush.'

As soon as he'd moved away, Splodge shot out and streaked towards the cat-flap. It swung in and out behind him, clattering. I hesitated, wondering whether to go after him. Now he was out in the darkness, part of it, swallowed up by it.

'It's Leo,' I said. 'Leo's scared him.'

And me. *I'd* scared him.

'Leave it now. At least you found him,' Mum said. 'I'll put his food down and he can have it later. He'll come in when we've all gone to bed.' She gave a big yawn. 'Gosh, I'm tired. Jennie had me up three times last night. Won't it be nice when she sleeps straight through? And Josh, look at the time. *You* ought to be in bed by now.'

We all heard the sound from the baby monitor. A few whimpers, a small hiccupping sound, a wail, then full-scale crying. So it *was* on, and they must have heard me with Jennie. Mum set off up the stairs, slow and weary like someone trudging up the last steps to the summit of Ben Nevis. I followed, too ashamed to say I was sorry, or even to say goodnight properly.

I'd said what I'd said, and it was impossible to unsay. But worst of all was that I hadn't even *meant* it. For those few seconds, something had got into me, taken over.

15
TIGER

On Thursdays, Mr Baynton takes our class for English. Really he's a Geography teacher, and Mrs Lloyd's our English teacher, but Mr Baynton has to do this one lesson a week because of a timetabling clash. He's called Blinky because he always blinks a lot, especially if he gets wound up. Sometimes he takes off his glasses and dabs at his eyes with a hanky. First time I saw this, I thought he was crying.

He was doing Poems. Today he read us this poem called *The Tiger,* which is so famous that I'd heard it before – the one that goes:

> *Tiger, tiger, burning bright*
> *In the forests of the night,*
> *What immortal hand or eye*
> *Could frame thy fearful symmetry?*

When he'd read it to us, he told us what some of the words mean, like *symmetry* and *sinews* and *anvil,* and then he asked us some questions about it. What did we think of it? What did we like about it?

There was a silence. Then Toby said, without putting his hand up, 'This William Blake bloke who wrote it, he must have run out of ideas.'

Mr Baynton blinked at him. 'How d'you work that out?'

Toby did this wind-up thing, opening his eyes very wide, then blinking just enough to make his friends laugh, without making it obvious enough for anyone to accuse him of taking the mick. The weird thing is, I've noticed Mr Baynton blinks a lot less when he's teaching Geography. It's English, and specially poems, that make him blink.

'Well,' said Toby. ''Sobvious. The end's exactly the same as the beginning. He couldn't think how to end it, so he's just copied out the beginning again.'

'And what does that do?' Mr Baynton was dabbing at one eye with his little finger.

Floss put up her hand, but before Blinky could ask her, Chad Wilkins joined in. 'It doesn't even rhyme. I mean, *eye* doesn't rhyme with that word *symmetry,* does it? Unless you say *symmetr-eye.* Rubbish, isn't it?'

'It's a sort of rhyme. A near-rhyme.' Mr Baynton took off his glasses, rubbed the lenses with his hanky, and put them on again. 'Poets do that, sometimes. Yes, er, Florence, isn't it?'

'Floss,' said Floss.

'Dental,' muttered Bex.

'See, Toby, I think you've missed the point of that verse,' said Floss, turning round to explain. 'It gives it a kind of frame. Brings us back to the start. Like we're back where we were, still wondering.'

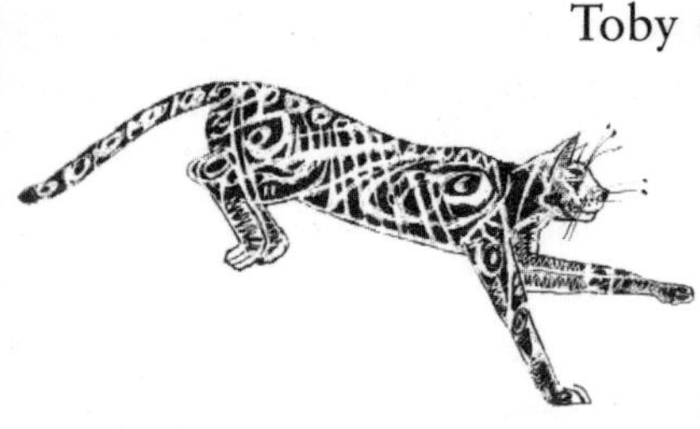

Toby made a *yeah, and?* face, but Blinky did a lot of nodding, and tried to get other people to join in. Course, now that Toby had rubbished the poem, and only Floss had put her hand up, no one else was keen, so he told us a bit about rhetorical questions and then asked us to make a list of adjectives. When we'd done that, we had to write our own poem about a tiger.

I didn't like it. I couldn't write about tigers *here,* in the classroom, with everyone else having a go at them. Cats are my private thing, and it didn't feel right even thinking about them in a lesson, surrounded by other people. For a few minutes I considered doing a Jamie-like sulk – refusing to do anything at all. I could always say I hadn't been able to think of anything.

Then I remembered doing list poems with Mrs Lloyd, last term. I could do one of those. So I wrote:

<u>The Tiger (panthera tigris)</u>

Tigers are immensely strong and powerful.
Tigers can bring down animals of ten times their own weight.
Tigers weigh between 130–189 kgs, and most of this is muscle.
Tigers grow to about 90 cms tall.
Tigers prey on herbivores, especially spotted deer.
Tigers eat up to 5 kgs at one meal and up to 25 kgs each day.
Tigers usually kill every 3–4 days.

Tigers live from 15–20 years.
Tigers breed at the end of the monsoon season and into winter.
Tigers (female) gestate their cubs for about 105 days.
Tigers give birth to 3–6 cubs.
Tiger cubs often don't survive though.

While I was finishing it, Blinky came and read it over my shoulder in the way I wish teachers wouldn't (it's even worse when you're doing a test, and they sneak up silently behind you). 'Did you really have all that information in your head, Latin names and all,' he asked me, 'or have you got an encyclopaedia in your bag?'

'Doesn't need one,' Brody told him. 'He's got an encyclopaedia for a brain.'

'That's quite amazing, Josh, and I wish I had your memory,' Mr Baynton went on. 'But it's not very – well – *poetic*, is it? Perhaps you could – er – add something. Try to use your imagination.'

He's basically OK, Mr Baynton, but that thing about using your imagination really gets me. I mean, *how* do you use it? Where do you keep it, and where does it go when you're *not* using it?

I started again. Five minutes later, Blinky called out, 'Time's almost up! Let's hear a couple of your poems. Who wants to go first? Octavia?'

Octavia Foskett wears sparkly hair-slides and very shiny shoes and keeps her pens and pencils in a fluffy pink pencil-case. She's got a little-girly voice that you can hardly hear, and the way she read her poem made it sound like a nursery rhyme.

'Tiger, tiger, fierce and strong,
Tiger, tiger, striped and bright,
Tiger, tiger, rare and special
Tiger, run with all your might.'

Mr Baynton nodded. 'Thank you, Octavia, that's very good indeed, and you've even made it rhyme. Who next?'

'Dental's got her hand up,' pointed out Toby. 'Ask her, she knows all about tigers. She's from Sarth Effrica.'

'Who? – er, oh yes. Florence, er, Floss. Thank you.'

Floss gave Toby a withering look. 'Tigers don't come from Africa. Don't you know anything?' Then she looked down at her draft book. 'I'm still working on it, but this will give you the idea.' She read out, very clearly:

'Who can know a tiger's mind?
Who can pace on tiger feet?
Who can see the forest shadows
Through a tiger's fiery eyes?
Who can know a tiger's heart?
Who can dream a tiger's dreams?

'And that's as far as I've got,' she said, in a different, more ordinary voice.

'Well,' said Mr Baynton, 'that's certainly an original approach. Thank you, er, Floss, for sharing that with us. I hope you all noticed how she used rhetorical questions, just like in Blake's poem. Well, time's up now! You can finish these off for homework, and we'll look at them again next week.'

'I've got one!' Toby's hand was up now.

'Go on then,' said Mr Baynton. Honestly, some teachers never learn.

Toby paused to make sure everyone was listening. Then he read out:

'Tiger, tiger, tiger rug,
Staring with your ugly mug,
There's not a lot that you can do
When people wipe their feet on you.'

There was an eruption of laughing. Chad overdid it, rocking back on his chair and clutching his stomach. He overbalanced, then grabbed at Toby one side and the radiator the other, just about saving himself. I turned round to Toby, and said, 'Tiger rugs? Yuk! And *ugly mug*? Look who's talking!' Only I don't think he heard me – he was too busy lapping up the attention.

'Fine, well that ends the lesson on a lighter note.' Mr Baynton was collecting his books together. 'See you for Geography. And I don't want any excuses about homework this time, Chad.'

As we made our way down to the Old Building for Art, Floss tagged along with Noori and Brody and me.

'That was a crap lesson,' she said. 'He does try, that Mr Baynton, but he's not good with poetry.'

'What, you're an expert, I s'pose?' Brody huffed.

'No, I mean, he didn't even ask us what the poem was *about*. What it *said* about tigers.'

'Tell you what, you take the lesson next time!'

Floss gave up with Brody, and fell into step next to me. 'How come you know so much?'

'I'm into animals. Specially big cats,' I told her. I put

some *what's-it-to-you?* into the way I said it, but she didn't notice.

'Me too!' she said, like that instantly made us best friends. 'We spent three weeks in the South Kruger last year. It was brilliant! We stayed in a safari lodge. We saw lions and leopards and a rhino there, and all kinds of things.'

'What, exactly?'

'Oh – elephants, zebra, waterbuck – and hyena, and loads of birds, like bee-eaters and hornbills and stuff, and klipspringer. You know what, you should go!'

'Some chance!' What, did she think we were millionaires or something? I had about as much chance of going to the South Kruger as I did of going on a space-shuttle holiday.

'You can look up the website —'

'Joshnfloss! Joshnfloss! Arr, how sweet are you two!'

I turned round to see Bex making kissy-kissy faces, and Toby pretending to put his fingers down his throat.

'What is it with those two? Why are they so stupid?' Floss asked me, quite seriously.

'Because they are. Look, see you later. Er, your, you know . . . poem. I thought it was, you know, good.'

'Hey, thanks!' She looked delighted.

I hurried to catch up with Noori and Brody, and made sure I got the seat next to Brody in the Art room. Floss went to sit with Sophie Cheung and Katie Williams at a different table, and I ignored her for the rest of the day.

16
JUNGLE

We had PE last thing, so I was a bit later than usual getting to St Luke's. Most of the mums and kids had gone, but through Jamie's classroom window I saw two people in there, talking. Mr Rose, and Mum.

Brody nudged me. 'Hey, look – I bet your brother's gone mental again!'

'Shut it, will you?' I said, through clenched teeth.

Noori, the peacemaker, wasn't with us today – he'd gone to the dentist. Brody looked surprised at how angry I'd sounded, and the truth was I'd surprised myself, too.

'Hey, cool it,' he said. 'Just joshing.'

His idea of a joke, that is. I've only heard it about twenty million times.

I told him, 'Well, don't josh with me, OK? Not about that.'

Brody shrugged. His little sister, Angie, was waiting for him by the gate. 'See you,' he called, and went on home.

I couldn't see Jamie. I went through the double doors to

the corridor, then saw him sitting at the back of the cloakroom, zipped into his anorak with his woolly hat pulled down nearly over his eyes. He was kicking his feet, banging them against the bench.

'Hi, Jamie!' I said. He didn't answer, of course, just looked at me from under the rolled brim of his hat, then down at his feet.

I could hear what Mr Rose was saying to Mum. 'It's completely unlike him, this kind of behaviour.'

'Thank you for letting me know,' Mum said. 'Do phone me straight away tomorrow, if anything —'

'I will,' said Mr Rose. He came to the door while she pushed the buggy through, and gave a tight little smile when he saw me there with Jamie. 'Bye, then. Have a good evening. See you tomorrow, Jamie.'

'Oh, hello, Josh,' Mum said to me. 'Come on then, Jamie.'

Jamie looked at her sulkily and heaved himself to his feet. A happy gurgling sound came from Jennie's buggy, but no one else looked cheerful.

'What's wrong?' I asked Mum, when we were all outside.

'Jamie's been in trouble.' She bent down to adjust the cover on the buggy. 'He's still not talking, but he seemed all right when I brought him back from the doctor's. Now Mr Rose says he broke Arran's new coloured pencils – snapped them in half, every one! – and he scratched Arran's hand when he tried to get them back. And since then he's been quite impossible. Behaving like a three-year-old.'

Jamie was trailing behind us. If he heard what Mum said, he showed no sign of it.

'Oh.' I wasn't sure whether this was progress or not. Being naughty on purpose, scratching people – that wasn't Jamie. He'd never done anything like that before. And Arran was his best friend.

This *wasn't* Jamie. It was Leo. I had a weird feeling of something crawling under my skin.

'What about the mask?' I said. 'He's not wearing it today.'

'No.' Mum looked round to check he was keeping up. 'He had it on at Dr Awan's – it was the only way I could get him to talk to her. He told her that Leo was fine. And he had it on when I left him at school at lunchtime. But Mr Rose says he took it off when he was supposed to finish the play with Arran, and wouldn't join in. Wouldn't cooperate at all.'

'He did yesterday,' I said. 'He talked yesterday. It's like he's frightened of what Leo might say.'

Mum shook her head. 'I don't know. I really don't know. I'll have another go at talking to him at home, with or without the mask. We're going the long way round, by the shops, to buy new pencils for Arran, then we're taking them to his house. You go on home, if you'd rather.'

The nearest shops are in the high street. We went into Smith's, and I bought two Pilot pens, and Mum chose a really nice set of pencils for Arran. I wondered if Jamie would have to pay for them out of his pocket money, or whether he'd get away with it, the way he seemed to be getting away with lots of things lately. He showed no interest, staring across the street, pushing out his lower lip. Half of me wanted to shake some sense into him, but the other half was really worried. What if we never got our normal Jamie back again? Where had he gone?

Mum had to buy a birthday card for her friend Claire. I knew she'd spend ages choosing, so I wandered over to look at the magazines. Jamie stayed with Mum, still with that babyish scowl on his face, just standing there looking at nothing. If he wanted attention, he wasn't going to get it from me.

'Hi, Josh,' said a voice. 'Thought it was you.'

I turned round, and there was Floss. We're meant to wear plain coats for school, black or navy, but Floss had this patterned knitted thing with red zig-zags across it, and a bright red scarf and hat. I suppose, being new, she was allowed to wear it till she got a dull boring coat like everyone else's.

'Is that your mum?' she asked me. 'And your little brother? He looks cute.'

I scuffed my shoe against the bottom magazine shelf and gave a Kevin-like mumble in reply.

'Are you going home now?' Floss went on. 'Cos I live quite near you, in Lansdowne Avenue. You're in Landsdowne Crescent, aren't you?'

Mum was at the checkout now, paying. She looked round for Jamie, and saw me with Floss. I started thinking about my Book of Cats, which is what I do when I don't want to be somewhere. It's like I can hide in it, just by thinking.

But Floss hadn't finished yet. When we left the shop, she tagged along.

'Hello!' she said to Mum. 'I'm Floss Darrow. I'm in Josh's class.' And she actually held out her hand to shake Mum's.

Mum looked surprised, because Floss is taller and looks older than me, and wasn't in proper school uniform, but they did the handshaking thing like business people at a meeting. 'Hello, I'm Josh's mum. This is Jamie, and baby Jennie.'

'Hi there, Jamie,' said Floss. Then she bent down to the buggy. 'Hello there, Jennie, how are you?' You'd have thought she seriously expected Jennie to answer. 'She's gorgeous, isn't she? You're so lucky, Josh. I'd love a baby brother or sister. I'm an only child, and I'm OK with that, but it'd be really cool to have a baby in the family.'

I could see that Mum was well impressed with Floss and her good manners. Mum's always going on about Noori, how polite he is, how he always says *thank you* and *please,* and calls her Mrs Bowman, and whenever he's going home from our house he thanks her and Mike for having him. 'Such a *nice* boy, Noori is. I'm glad you're friends with him.' You'd think I was a total slob, compared. I knew she'd say, later on, 'Such a *nice* girl, that Floss is. I'm glad you're friends with her.'

We set off home, Floss with us. When we got to the corner of Harcourt Drive, where Arran lives, Mum and Jamie and the buggy turned right. Mum gave me the key, and I walked on with Floss. All I needed now was Bex or Toby to come by on the bus.

I was wondering how soon I could get rid of her, when she said, 'See this.' She took a screwed-up piece of paper out of her coat pocket, and handed it to me. I unfolded it, and read:

Dental, dental, dental Floss
We think U R total dross
What we see is what we get
UR such a teacher's pet
Y don't U shut your gr8 big mouth
Go back home to Africa (South)

'Who gave you this?' I asked, though I could guess.

'No one *gave* it to me. I found it in my coat pocket after PE. It's that Bex girl, isn't it, and Toby?'

'It's just a joke, I expect,' I said. 'They'll get tired of it soon.'

Floss frowned. 'But why do they do it? I've tried to be friendly.'

'It's just – anyone who's new, they'll try to wind them up. Specially if there's anything, well, different about you. With you it's cos you talk different and there's lots of stuff you don't know about school yet. And it's cos you're, you know, quite brainy. Just ignore them.'

I sounded just like my dad. We'd had conversations like this.

Floss was striding along the pavement so fast that I had to scuttle to keep up, then wondered why I was bothering. 'OK,' she said, 'so I'm brainy. So are you. So's Noori. What's wrong with that?'

'It's like, if you're clever, you have to hide it a lot of the time,' I told her. 'You don't have to keep putting your hand up. It helps if you sometimes act a bit thick. Noori's OK, cos he's quiet. No one bothers him. So's Sophie Cheung, and she comes top in everything.'

'I don't get it! How come Bex and Toby get to decide what's allowed and what's not? There are what, twenty-eight other kids in the class?'

'Right, but those two are the loudest. They make more noise than the other twenty-six.'

'My mum warned me it might be hard,' Floss said. 'School's a jungle, she said. She hated it, when she was my age. She got bullied. That's why she taught me at home.'

'So what made you want to start school, then?' I still couldn't get my head round this.

'I wanted to meet other kids. And now I am. I'll be OK. I can deal with it.'

'Look —' I didn't quite know how to put this. What I really meant was, if she stopped acting like she thought she was better than everyone else, people might be friendlier. 'Even Chad isn't as thick as he pretends. It's not cool to be all that interested in lessons. You could pretend to be bored sometimes. Here's where I live.'

'OK. Thanks. D'you want to come round, some time? To ours, I mean. We're only round the corner.'

'Dunno,' I mumbled. 'I'm a bit busy.'

I let myself in. It was a bit much, having to be Floss's agony uncle. I'd got enough problems of my own.

At home, Jamie put on his Leo mask only briefly, told Mum what he wanted for tea, then took it off and didn't speak all evening.

Something had got into the house, something that made me not want to be there. Mum and Mike were obviously worried, but trying not to show it. Whenever Mum spoke to me, it was in a fake breezy way, like she wanted to pretend everything was normal. I did my Maths and Geography homework, then went up to the bedroom and spent some time on my Book of Cats. I stuck in the 'Tiger' poem (William Blake's, not my unpoetic one) and drew a picture to put with it. Then I had an idea for a better poem of my own, so I wrote that down. I was quite pleased with it, so I copied it out and stuck it into the book as well.

When Mum brought Jamie up at bedtime, I'd had enough of the fake-cheerful stuff, so I went to the computer. It was in the spare room, the room that was going to be Jennie's. It was wedged in near the door, on its little table, because the rest of the room was taken up with boxes and piles of stuff that need sorting. I was still there when I heard Mum talking to Dad on the phone, from her bedroom.

'I'm taking him on Monday . . . yes . . . are you tied up? A-huh – I know – yes. Well, how about Saturday? Can you come over? A-huh. A-huh.' (Mum always does a lot of this *a-huh*ing on the phone.) 'Right, yes. Oh, Josh is fine! He's made friends with a girl from his class – yes, she's new, from South Africa – It's good Josh is helping her settle in – fine, I'll give him a shout, hang on, I think he's on the computer —'

She brought me the phone. Dad was doing it too, the fake-jolly 'So, how's things? What's this about a girlfriend, hey?'

'Dad! She's not a girlfriend. Just someone in my class. We bumped into her on the way home. Don't even know if I like her.'

'Just winding you up,' said Dad. 'I'll see you on Saturday. I'm coming over in the afternoon.'

'What, with Kevin? And Kim?' I didn't want Kevin *here,* with his grumpy face and shifting eyes! Even saying his name made me bad-tempered.

'No, no. Just me. Josh, I know you're being a big help to Mum. Good boy. Big help to Jamie, too. You will understand, won't you, if I spend a bit of time with Jamie on our own – maybe take him out somewhere? But we'll have a chat, too.'

'Yeah, whatever.' I knew he hated me saying that. 'D'you want Mum again?'

But now, from Mum's bedroom, I heard Jennie starting to cry – a rising wail that would soon be full-scale yelling.

'Sounds like your little sister needs attention,' Dad said. 'No, it's OK. Night, then, Josh. See you Saturday.'

'Josh? Why aren't you in bed?' Mum called above the racket of bawling baby. She was using her tired, cross voice that I didn't like. 'You ought to be getting ready by now. I've been too busy with Jamie and Jennie to notice the time.'

'No, no, don't worry about me,' I grumped to myself, turning off the computer. 'I'm fine. No, really.'

Mum was all Jamie, Jamie, Jamie. Jennie, Jennie, Jennie. And Dad would have Kevin. Who'd have time for *Josh*?

Soon Kevin would be with Dad every day, and Jamie and me only every other weekend. He'd act like the house was *his,* and we were unwanted visitors. Like the computer's his and the TV's his. Or I'd be in the bathroom, and Kevin would thump on the door, and what if I'd made a smell? I'd have to open the door and come out, and he'd go in and smell my smell, and he'd do that sneery face he does, to show I'm not just a geeky little kid he's got to put up with, I'm disgusting as well. How was I meant to cope with that?

Jamie was asleep – or at least I thought he was. The cat

mask was where he'd left it, on the low table between our beds. I turned on the bedside lamp, and picked it up. By now it was a bit crumpled, and torn where the elastic was attached, but still recognisable as Leo.

I held it up to my face and looked through the slits. Then I slipped the elastic over my head and stood up to look at myself in the mirror.

'I'm Leo,' I said, in the drawly voice Jamie had used. 'Leo. Don't try to tell me what to do. I do whatever I want.'

Partly, I was mucking about – but partly, I wasn't. And as I looked at my reflection, a shivery thrill went through me. He was there. He'd been there all the time.

Leo looked back at me. Striped, solemn face. Alert ears. Deep, mysterious eyes. My eyes, lion eyes. I felt bigger, prouder, stronger than my Josh self, as big as a lion. I stared and stared. In the dim light of the bedroom, he – I – *we* – looked fierce and dramatic. A lion lurking in shadows. Who knew what was going on in his – in our – lion mind?

The bed creaked, and a movement in the mirror made me turn. Jamie was sitting up in bed, staring at me. His eyes were wide and round.

'Josh?' he said. 'Make him go away! Please – *make him go away*!'

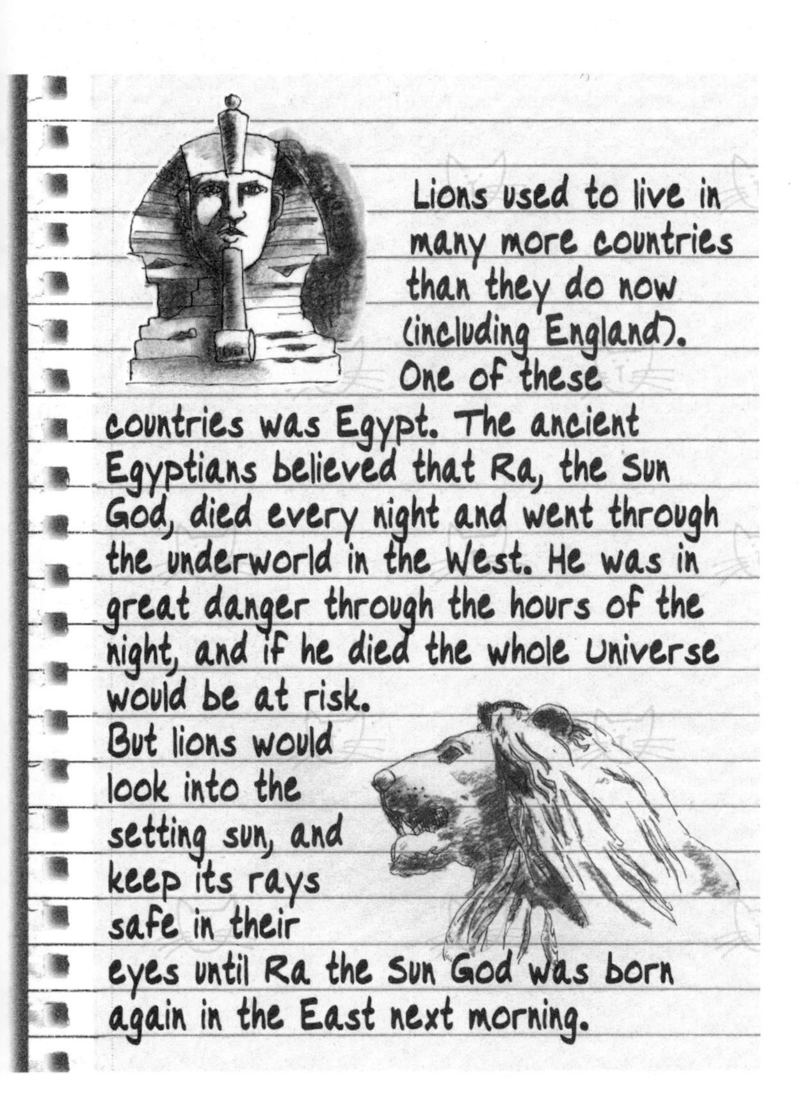
Lions used to live in many more countries than they do now (including England). One of these countries was Egypt. The ancient Egyptians believed that Ra, the Sun God, died every night and went through the underworld in the West. He was in great danger through the hours of the night, and if he died the whole Universe would be at risk.
But lions would look into the setting sun, and keep its rays safe in their eyes until Ra the Sun God was born again in the East next morning.

17
PROWLER

Something had got into the house.

It crept into my bed, making me restless and uncomfortable. It seeped into my body, making me fidgety and hot. It oozed into my brain, making me edgy and fearful. When I slept, wildcats roamed through my dreams and clawed at the insides of my eyelids. When I was awake, they lurked in the shadows of the room. Once, my eyes jerked open and I looked straight at Jamie. He was sitting up in bed, staring back at me. And, weird though this was, I must have dozed off again, because next time I woke up, the Something was coming straight at me.

My heart was thumping so loudly that it made my hands shake. It took me three tries to find the lamp-switch.

The prowling thing was Jamie. At once he stopped dead. He'd been sneaking up on me, caught in the light, freeze-framed.

In that moment, I was scared of him – the look on his face was so weird, so unJamielike.

'Jamie?' My voice wobbled out. 'What's up? What d'you *want*?'

He didn't answer. Eyes fixed on mine, he started to move forward, very slowly. It was like Splodge in the garden, when he sees a bird and stalks it in slow motion: one front leg reaching forward, then a pause for concentration. Splodge's whole body would be focused on that bird, just as the whole of Jamie's body was focused now. On what? What did he want from me?

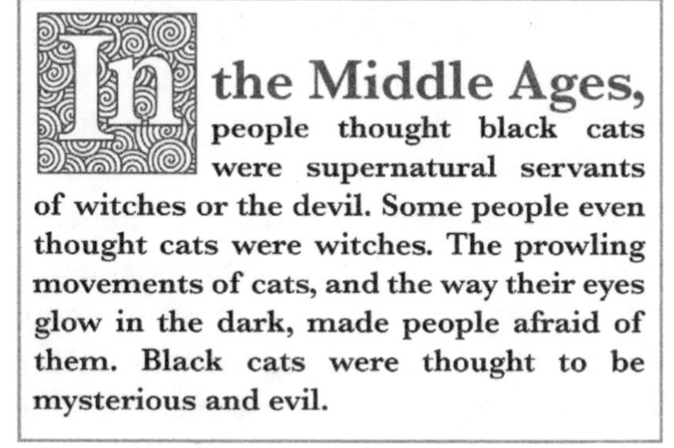

In the Middle Ages, people thought black cats were supernatural servants of witches or the devil. Some people even thought cats were witches. The prowling movements of cats, and the way their eyes glow in the dark, made people afraid of them. Black cats were thought to be mysterious and evil.

I clutched my pillow. The light in the room seemed too bright to be real, Jamie's pyjamas too blue, his eyes too bright and fixed. I thought of Brody saying, 'He's gone mental again, your brother.' What if he had? What if he was possessed by Leo – what if he was really losing it? I didn't like the thought of this person, this Jamie-but-not-Jamie, creeping round the room while I was asleep. Watching me. Stalking me. Goose-pimples prickled my arms and neck. Whatever Leo-strength I'd had earlier had drained out of me. I'd shrunk smaller than Jamie.

The fear grabbed hold. With both arms, I hurled my

pillow at him. 'Stop it! Stop acting stupid and get back in bed!'

The pillow hit him full in the face. He stumbled against the wardrobe door, then slumped to the floor. I expected him to yell out, and Mum to come stomping in and demand to know what was going on, but he didn't make a sound.

I shouldn't have done it. But I had.

'Stop it! Stop mucking about!' I swung my feet to the floor and went to help him up. 'Do you want the toilet or something? What's with this stupid Leo performance?'

I'd got hold of his arm, but he resisted and made himself limp. He looked up at me and I saw his eyes shiny with tears. Then, slowly, like a very old man, he got up and went back to his bed. He got in and pulled the duvet over himself.

'You all right?'

'No!' He looked at me, then whispered, 'Make him go away.' He was holding Lowther, not noticing that he was upside-down.

'Make *who* go away?'

'Leo. Make Leo go away.'

'But you like Leo,' I told him.

'I don't! He gets inside me and won't go away.'

'For God's sake!' I burst out. 'We've all had it with Leo – give it a rest, can't you?'

He gave a big sniffle, and clutched Lowther more tightly.

'At least you're *talking* now,' I said, in a nicer voice. 'Bet you could have talked all along.'

Jamie shook his head. 'He's real,' he whimpered. 'He gets inside me and burns me with his breath.'

'No. He doesn't. You're making it up —'

'He does! He does!'

A tear brimmed over and splashed down his cheek. No, he wasn't pretending. Whatever it was, it was real enough to him. It had been real to me, too, when I looked in the mirror. And just now.

'All right, Jame.' I swallowed hard. 'I'll – I'll try to make him go away.'

I looked at my cube clock. Nearly half past six. The first feeble grey light was starting to push through the darkness outside. Half an hour till it was time to get up. I could hear Mum moving about now, murmuring to Jennie. The cat mask was where I'd hidden it last night, under my bed. Was that what Jamie had been looking for?

But he was talking now. As Jamie.

I wondered whether to call out to Mum, but instead I looked at him intently and said, 'Jamie. What did the lion tell you?'

An obstinate expression came over his face. 'Nothing. Lions don't talk.'

'That one did, the one we saw. He said something to you, didn't he?'

Jamie shook his head vigorously. 'No! Lions don't talk, stupid!'

And then Mum was in our room, wrapping her dressing-gown round her, looking at us first in amazement and then in delight, when she saw that Jamie wasn't wearing the Leo mask.

'I thought I heard you talking! Oh —' She came over and kissed Jamie, then me. 'How are you feeling today, J?'

Jamie shrugged. 'I'm OK.' He made it into a question, *why are you asking?* 'Can we have porridge?'

'Yes, if you want. You get in the shower while I change Jennie, then I'll go down and make it. All right?'

I could tell she didn't want to push Jamie by asking too many questions, but she gave me a *well done* look and went back to her own room.

'Jamie —' I began, wondering whether to ask him again about the lion, but he got in first, sounding perfectly normal.

'Who are Chelsea playing on Saturday? Do you know?'

'Arsenal, isn't it?'

It didn't seem the right moment for lions. When he went to have his shower, I pulled out the mask – just a tatty piece of card with crayoning on it, that's all it was – and took it into Mum's room. That was Leo out of the way. Mike was still in bed, fast asleep – all I could see was one eyebrow and a tuft of hair. Mum had finished changing Jennie's nappy, and was settling her back in her cot.

'Here.' I handed her the mask. 'Jamie wants Leo to go away. So p'raps we shouldn't have this in our room. But I didn't bin it, just in case he wants it again.'

'Wants Leo to go away? Is that what he said?'

I nodded.

'Thanks, Josh. I'll keep this. I might want to show it to the psychologist. There, that's you sorted out, young madam,' she said to Jennie. 'Now – porridge.'

'Yes please,' Mike said, without opening his eyes.

18
MENTAL

Friday turned out to be one of those days when nothing seems to go right. One of those days when everything gangs up on you. One of those days that seems bad and unfair from the start. When anything that can go wrong, *will* go wrong. Once you know you're having that kind of day, the only thing is to get through to bedtime and hope tomorrow will be back to normal.

First thing was, I hadn't done my French homework. I'd forgotten all about it. And if you're going to turn up to any teacher's lesson without your homework, you'd better not choose Mr Dawkins.

'Did I imply to you that homework was an optional extra?' he went.

'No, but —'

'Did I ask you to do it as a special favour to me?'

'No, but —'

'Did I suggest that homework might be available to liven up those dull moments when you find yourself with nothing better to do?'

I gave up trying to answer, and dumbly shook my head.

He *enjoys* going on like this, I swear he does. It's a sort of performance. He must have got a real kick from standing over me like a one-man Gestapo, while Toby and Bex and Chad giggled in the back row.

'In that case, I cannot understand why you have no work to hand in. Maybe you'd care to explain.'

'Forgot,' I mumbled.

'He's having a hard time at home, sir,' Bex called out helpfully.

What? I turned round to glare poison darts at her.

It worked, though. You could see Mr Dawkins thinking, what, parents splitting up? (No, done that.) Dad lost his job? (No, been there as well.) House flooded out, or struck by lightning? Someone died? He backed off.

'See me at the end of the lesson then, Josh,' he said, and started on about verbs that go with *être*.

After I'd stayed behind for a large dose of *one more time's a detention* and *you need to adjust your attitude,* I steamed off down the corridor, ignoring Brody and Noori, who'd waited for me outside. I was looking for Bex. I knew where she hung out with Freya at break and lunchtimes, in the canteen, waiting for a year ten boy they both fancied. There was Bex, leaning against the door-frame, to give her victim no chance of escape.

'What was that about?' I shouted as soon as I saw her.

'What?'

'In French just now. Hard time at home.'

She put on a prissy face. 'Only trying to help. Don't thank me or anything, though.'

'Who asked you?'

'Don't go on at *her*,' said Freya, champing crisps. 'Just

cos your brother's a mental case. She got Dawkins off your back, didn't she?'

'A *what*?'

'Don't worry.' Bex had out her mobile now and was texting away with both thumbs. 'He's going to a mental clinic, isn't he? They'll give him drugs and stuff, sort him out, I expect.'

Freya looked at me, smirking. 'Does it run in the family?'

'Where d'you get all that rubbish from?' I demanded.

'From him!' Bex tilted her head towards Brody.

Right. Got it. Brody's little sister's in the same class as Jamie, and so's Bex's brother. They'd know how weird Jamie had been, and Brody knew about the psychologist. Didn't expect him to blab it all round the class, though, or I'd never have told him.

I swivelled round to Brody.

'What?' he said, all innocence. 'You didn't say it was secret!'

I don't know what got hold of me then. I hurled my bag at the nearest table and flew at Brody, grabbed him by his coat and shoved him as hard as I could, throwing my whole weight at him. Off-balance, he stumbled against a chair, which tipped and crashed to the floor. We both fell, me half on top of him, wanting to punch and wrench and hurt. I was vaguely aware of the commotion around us, Noori trying to pull me away, Bex's voice chanting, '*Fight! Fight! Fight!*' other kids either hurrying over or scattering out of our way, and then, cutting through it all, a teacher's voice: 'Hey! Stop that! Right now!'

Getting to my feet, I felt a trickle of blood down my shin. Must have scraped it on the chair. My bag, where I'd chucked it, had toppled another chair over. A small crowd had gathered, first to watch the fight, now for the fun of seeing me and Brody getting an earful. I didn't know the name of the duty teacher, the one who'd shouted out, but now Mr O'Shea was striding into the canteen. It'd have to be him, wouldn't it? The other teacher spoke to him quietly, and Mr O'Shea rapped at us, 'You boys! Up to my study. *Now.*'

In the admin corridor, we were left standing outside Rick's closed door while the two teachers talked inside.

'Thanks a lot!' Brody hissed at me.

'Well, you asked for it!'

'Asked for it *how?* You're mental, you are – total headcase, just like —'

'Shut it! Just shut it! I'll get you, later!'

And, course, that was the moment Mr O'Shea opened his door. He froze, looked at me, and told us both to come in.

Result: mega ear-bashing from Rick, along with a lot of head-shaking, and *utter disgrace,* and *shocked to hear of such behaviour,* and a threat to phone our parents if anything like this ever happened again, *and* a lunchtime detention for both of us. This took up the whole of break, so we were late for History, and had to explain to Mrs Cartwright, while Bex sniggered.

For the rest of the day, Noori tried to make peace between us, but I wasn't having it. I wouldn't speak to Brody. Hardly spoke to anyone, in fact. I suppose you could say I did a Jamie. Brody and I did our detention, and he had a go at talking afterwards, but I wouldn't listen.

Maths, Art and RE dragged by, and at last it was time for home. Only I didn't feel like going home. Brody set off for St Luke's as usual, jogging, keen to get away from me. I didn't go after him.

Didn't want to see Jamie, didn't want to see Mum. Didn't want to see anyone.

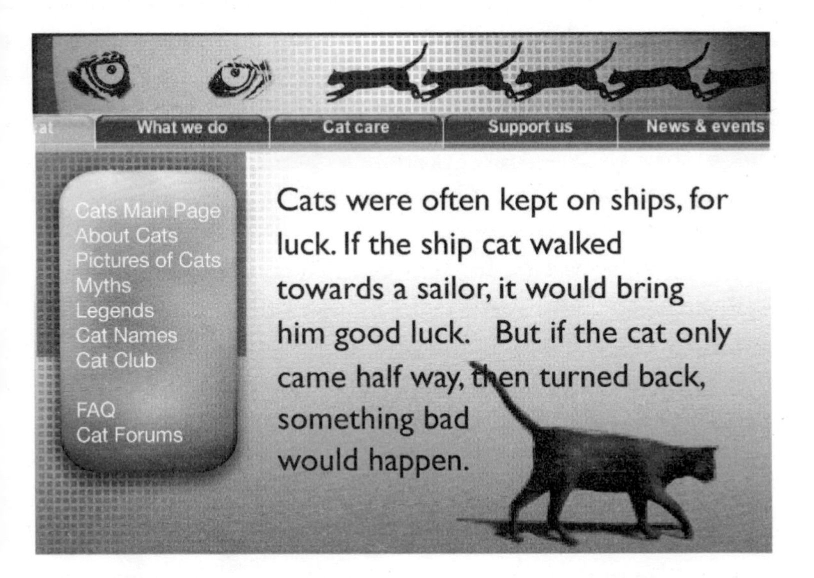

19
STRANGER DANGER

Noori was waiting for me, but I told him I had to go to the shops, and walked off before he had the chance to say he'd come too.

I hung around in the High Street for a bit, but there were loads of kids from school there, older ones flirting with each other, calling names across the street or pretending to push each other in front of buses. I decided to walk, and headed off without knowing where to go. A bus to Wembley pulled up at the next bus-stop, so I bought a ticket from the machine and jumped on just in time. I sat upstairs at the back. When everyone else got off, I did too, then walked some more.

Usually I like being out in the streets, especially in the mornings when the shops are opening up and the roads are busy with delivery vans and people going off to jobs and school. I like the feeling of the day starting up, and I like seeing people, wondering where they're going and what sort of day they're going to have.

This was different, though. I was making myself feel

like a runaway, a fugitive, because it suited my mood. It was already getting dark, and it was cold too, and starting to drizzle. I carried on walking, choosing whichever direction I liked the look of. Noise spilled out of a pub, and a man wavered across the pavement in front of me. I smelled fag-ash and whisky, even though it must be early for drinking. A group of big lads came towards me, laughing, taking up the whole pavement. The drunk man shouted something at a passing car, then one of the group yelled out something I didn't catch. There was a bit of laughing and shoving, and two of the boys barged into me, but didn't say sorry.

I turned left into a quieter street. It led away from the shops, into a road of parked cars and vans, and lock-up garages. There were rubbish bins and an overflowing skip. Should I carry on, or go back to the road with the pub in it? I had no idea where I was. There was no street sign that I could see, so I walked on till I saw some, but the names Wigley Road and Albion Crescent didn't mean anything to me. I carried on to the next corner. The rain was coming down harder now, and a passing motor-bike sprayed water all over my trousers. This was pointless, but I wasn't giving in and going home. Not yet. My hair was getting wet, and cold water was seeping down inside the neck of my coat. After a bit I almost started to enjoy it, in an odd way. It felt right, the mood I was in. An icy wind and a blast of hailstones would have been even better.

A right turn, then left and right again, brought me to another main street, with buses and cars and traffic lights. It was busy here, Friday rush hour, everyone coming home from work. I saw a warmly-lit café, Agnelli's Cappuccino Bar, and thought of going inside. It made me think of Mike, steaming and foaming away with his new coffee machine. I'd have loved one of his special choco-lattes just then.

Ahead of me I saw steps down into an Underground station. People were streaming out, turning up collars, zipping their coats, opening umbrellas. I went down and looked at the big map, with the tube lines all in different colours. I could get on the Bakerloo line here, then change for wherever I wanted. Where *did* I want? I stood tracing the Bakerloo brown with my finger, and saw that at Baker Street it links up with the yellow of the Circle Line. The Circle Line goes to South Kensington, which is where you get off for the Natural History Museum. I knew because we went there on a school trip once, and I wanted to see the Wildlife Photographer of the Year exhibition that was on now.

Dad had said he'd take Jamie and me one Saturday, but he hadn't yet. It'd be warm and dry in the museum, and I could stay there till it closed.

Then I remembered seeing on the website that the museum was free, but you had to pay to see the photography exhibition. I felt in my pocket to see if I had enough money. There was no note, only a lot of coins. While I was counting them, it dawned on me that even if I had enough to get in, it'd be pointless to go there as late as this, when I wouldn't have time to see everything.

A man was standing next to me – had been for a few moments – and I realised that he wasn't looking at the map, but at me. When I noticed him, he grinned. If he thought he knew me, I didn't recognise him. He was about Dad and Mike's age, in an overcoat, with a shirt and tie underneath.

'All right, son? Not lost, are you?'

'No. I'm fine.' Standing down here in the warmth and light, I shivered with the damp that clung to me. One of my shoes was leaking, my hair dripped, and the cold trickle inside my coat made me want to be safely indoors. I was hungry, too, but if I spent my money on a McDonald's I might not have enough to pay for a bus home.

I went up to the street again, thinking I might buy a bar of chocolate at least, then look for a bus. When I stopped to look round for a paper shop, I saw that the man had followed me up the steps. He grinned at me again, and came over.

'If you're short of dosh, I'll help you out,' he told me.

'Give you a lift somewhere, if you want. Where you trying to get to?'

How dim did he think I was? There was no way I was getting in a car with a man I didn't know. And I didn't like the way he was smiling at me. But there were lots of other people about, so I wasn't really worried.

'Nowhere,' I told him, and ran back down the steps. At the bottom I turned to make sure he hadn't followed me again, but he was just standing there watching.

Even though I wasn't scared of him, it made me realise how alone I was, in a place I didn't know. How many times have Mum and Mike told me – always let them know where I'm going, and what time I'll be back? They'd be furious. I counted out change for the ticket machine and bought a single child ticket, then got on a Metropolitan Line train westbound. By now I wished I'd never thought of this. I was tired and hungry and damp, and I hadn't been to the Natural History Museum or run away from home or done anything dramatic at all. I felt like a wuss.

The train was full of rush-hour people, and I had to stand all the way to our stop. Then the ten-minute walk home. A blue Focus was parked outside – that meant Mum's friend Claire was visiting.

'Josh! Where've you been?' Mum's face was bright and relieved. 'And you're soaked, look at you!'

'Went round someone's house.' I tried to make it sound like nothing.

'*Whose* house? Why didn't you phone? I've been worried. Come on, get those wet things off. Let me hang your coat up.' I dumped my rucksack and followed her through to the kitchen. They were having a cup of tea there, and Claire was holding Jennie. '*Whose* house?' Mum asked again. 'Was it that girl, Floss?'

'*No!* I went round to Noori's.' I crossed my fingers behind my back.

'Well, why didn't you say?'

I just shook my head. I knew Mum was crosser than she wanted to show in front of Claire.

When I'd changed into jeans and sweatshirt I went in the front room with Jamie and thawed out by the fire, and Mum brought me a glass of apple juice and a piece of walnut cake.

Jamie stared at me. 'Did you run away?'

So he was still talking, even if only in that odd dull way, as if he wasn't properly awake. Perhaps that meant we could forget about the psychologist.

'I just didn't feel like coming straight home, that was all!' I told him. 'I got on a bus and then a train. Only don't tell Mum.'

'Where would you go, though, if you did run away from home? Would you go to the zoo?'

I huffed a laugh. 'What, you think I'd find myself a nice cosy cage, and make myself a straw nest to sleep in? Look, I didn't run away, and I'm not going to, so what's the point of asking?'

'You'd need lots of money, I expect.'

'Yes, I expect you would,' I told him, picking up the remote to see what was on TV. 'And I haven't got lots of money, so I'd be stuck.'

'You could have taken your Christmas money. Have you still got it?'

'Yes, in my drawer. It's for my binoculars.'

'You could have bought a train ticket with that.'

'Yeah, but I didn't have it with me, and anyway I want the binoculars. Stop going on about it, OK?'

Mike came in soon after that, and Claire stayed for pasta and salad and they opened a bottle of wine, so Mum forgot she was in a nark with me. I felt bad about lying to her, but she didn't ask any more questions, so I didn't say anything. I was annoyed, too, that she hadn't been all *that* worried. I mean, I could have been kidnapped or murdered for all she knew, and she was too busy gossiping with Claire to notice!

Splodge crossed in front of me as I got to the top of the stairs, so maybe that would bring me better luck, whether it was the black or the white that did it. Tomorrow had to be a better day.

20
WHAT THE LION SAID

Going to bed, I thought of what Jamie had asked me. *Make him go away. Please, make him go away.*

I hadn't, though, had I? Jamie had asked me for help, and I hadn't given it. Instead, I was letting Leo take me over as well. Leo was here now, inside me, inside Jamie.

If he went away, what would he leave behind? Would he take part of Jamie with him? Part of me?

I shivered, thinking of cat eyes staring, eyes like drills that bored into my brain. Lion eyes, solemn, amber, unblinking.

I knew I was dreaming.

It wasn't winter but a hot, dry day in summer. The patio doors were wide open, and my feet were bare. I walked to the open door for coolness. There, in the garden, was Splodge, running towards me from the shrubs at the back, with something in his mouth. A small pale thing. An alive and writhing thing.

'Splodge! Drop it!'

I ran out, feeling the warm grass under my toes. Splodge backed off, glaring. A warning growl sounded in his throat. I saw the mouse clamped between his jaws – its bright eye, its quiver of whiskers, a feeble movement of one small paw. Splodge had changed – not a pet, a purring lap-sitter, but a wild, savage creature.

As I hesitated, wondering whether to shout loudly or make a grab and hope he'd drop the mouse, he changed even more. He grew and grew, filling the lawn. His black-and-white patches melted together and became tawny gold. A ragged mane sprouted around his neck. His paws were heavily padded, his legs were muscled. And all the time his amber eyes stared at me, holding me, reaching far inside me, telling me what he knew.

How could I have made such a stupid mistake? It wasn't our back garden after all, but the lion enclosure at the wildlife park. How could I have mistaken a full-grown lion for a pet cat? Where were the bars between us, the deep ditch? Where was Dad? There was nothing but air, and when I opened my mouth to shout for help, darkness rushed into my throat, clogging it tight.

What the lion carried in his mouth wasn't a mouse, either. It was bigger. It was wrapped in white baby clothes. I saw the movement of a podgy hand. I saw long, curved teeth, sunk into the baby blanket.

The lion's eyes burned into me, and I knew they were speaking. They were telling me what I already knew.

My throat, my lungs, my whole body was straining to yell out, '*No!*' The word stayed in my throat, choked. But someone else was screaming. It sliced the air into jagged strips, hurting my ears. Someone was screaming for me, voicing what I couldn't: 'No! *No! No!*'

Jamie.

I opened my eyes and saw the pale strip of street-light that was the gap between the curtains. Safe in my own bed. No lion. But Jamie –

'Jamie! Jamie! Wake up – you're all right!'

A flick of the light switch chased away the shadows. Jamie, whimpering, had clenched himself into a tight knuckle of fear under his duvet. Gently, I shook his shoulder.

'Jamie! It's all right! But I don't know what happened – I think I was dreaming your dream —'

Jamie uncurled enough to look at me. His eyes were swimming with tears. 'Lowther,' he said. 'I want Lowther.'

I looked round, and found Lowther on the floor where he'd fallen out of bed. When I picked him up, Jamie grabbed him and pulled him under the duvet.

I took a deep breath, and tried to find words.

'Jamie,' I said. 'It's the lion, isn't it? The lion we saw, all mixed up with Splodge and that mouse he killed? Is that what you dreamed? Jame, I saw him too! I dreamed the lion, with – with something in his mouth. He looked at me. But he spoke to you, didn't he? *What did he say?*'

Jamie's eyes closed. A tear trickled down the side of his face.

'He said – he said —'

'Yes?'

'He said, *I know. You don't want her, do you?*' His eyes opened. He gazed straight at me.

'Her?'

'The baby,' Jamie whispered. '*I'll get rid of her. For you. I'll get rid of her.*'

Floorboards creaked on the other side of the landing. Jamie's face twisted in misery. 'Don't tell Mum,' he whispered. 'Please! Promise you won't tell her! Don't tell anyone!'

So I promised.

But what now?

It meant that I was the only person who could help, didn't it? Unless the psychologist was a mind-reader.

Mike and I spent Saturday morning sorting out the junk room.

For the two years we'd lived here, this had been the place for shoving whatever didn't belong anywhere else. The computer and its chair stood just inside the door, but the rest of the room was a junk-hole. It was crammed full of Mike's golf clubs, and old jigsaw puzzles and games, and pictures that didn't have anywhere to hang, and crusted old paint tins, and things that might be useful if they were mended or oiled or given new batteries. The plan was to clear everything out and turn this into Jennie's bedroom. Till we did, it was so stuffed that we could only get in there by trampling and clambering and balancing. Splodge teetered on top of a pile of boxes, working out where to go next. He loved messy places, and boxes and bags he could hide in.

'We should have done this ages ago,' Mike said. 'We've got the wallpaper and the curtains. I've put off tackling this lot, that's the trouble.'

'How come Jennie gets a room to herself?' Jamie asked, appearing in the doorway. 'Me and Josh have to share.' Splodge turned and looked at him, then made a leap for the window-sill, scrabbling with his back legs for a grip. He pressed himself against the window and looked at Jamie with wide, round eyes.

'She's a girl. She'll need privacy when she's older.' Mike swayed, one foot in a space he'd cleared by the door, the other one groping for a foothold further in. Balanced, he turned to look at Jamie. 'I thought you *liked* sharing with Josh?'

There was a pause while Jamie thought about it. Then he said, 'I do,' in the flat, unJamielike voice we were getting used to.

'When I win the lottery,' Mike said, 'we'll have a loft conversion and bags of room. Indoor swimming-pool and jacuzzi as well. Here, Josh, take this. Got those bin bags?'

Before long, the landing was knee-deep in bags and boxes.

'What'll we do with all this?' I asked. Jamie had gone downstairs, and Splodge had come down from the window-sill and crawled inside a carrier-bag of old Christmas cards.

'Some can be stashed up in the loft, some can go to the charity shop, and I'll do a tip run with the rest,' Mike said. 'Or we could have a bonfire. There's all this old paperwork I should have slung out years ago. Can't think why I didn't dump it when we moved here.'

'Let's have it tonight, the bonfire!' I said. 'Dad'll be here.'

'Well, I suppose we could. It should be a clear night.'

I liked bonfires, especially in cold weather. I thought of flames leaping, and crackling twigs, and drifting flakes of ash. And that gave me an idea.

Dad was due to come over about three, because he'd been working all morning. Mum left Jennie with Mike and went to the supermarket to get sausages and potatoes for a bonfire supper. While she was out, and Mike busy with Jennie, Jamie and I went into the garden to collect bits of pruned twig for the fire. I took the chance to tell him my idea.

'You know when we were at the Wildlife Park?'

Of course he did. He said nothing, frowning.

'And I told you how humans first found a way of frightening lions?' I said.

'Fire!' Jamie was breaking off pieces of dry twig, not looking at me.

'That's right. They used fire. Lions are frightened of fire. What you ought to try, if Leo comes near you, if you want him to go away – what you do is, you imagine a great big fire, big flames jumping up between you and him. Then he can't get at you. If it's at night, and you're in bed, you can just turn the light on. The light'll frighten him away.'

Jamie looked obstinate. 'I'm not scared of lions. I'm not scared of anything.'

'OK, but – you, you know, asked me to help. So I'm trying.'

'Well, don't.' He hunched away from me. 'Why can't you leave me alone?'

21
SHADOWS

When Dad came, he brought Kevin with him. After he'd said he wasn't going to.

I heard him muttering excuses to Mum. 'Look, I know it's not ideal, but Kim had to stand in for someone ill at work, and Kevin's been helping me with a job this morning. It'll be OK. I thought I'd take Jamie to the park, on his own – Kev can stay here with Josh.'

Great. I suppose he thought Kevin and I were best mates.

Kevin was about as chatty as usual. While the grown-ups had a cup of tea, he sat in the corner listening to his Walkman and playing games on his mobile phone. At least it let me off the hook. When Dad and Jamie went out, Mum and Mike buzzed about the kitchen getting the food ready for later, and Kevin stayed plugged in to whatever he was doing.

I escaped upstairs to the bedroom. I needed to finish setting up the computer in there – connect the scanner and printer, and check that they still worked.

While I was doing this, the door-bell rang, and I heard Mike answering. Then he yelled up the stairs, 'Josh! Floss is here to see you!'

Floss? What was she doing here?

I turned everything off and went down. Floss was in the kitchen, with the others. All of them except Kevin were looking at Jennie, who was kicking on her mat, and Mum was pouring apple juice.

'Hi, Josh,' Floss said, as if it was quite normal to be in our kitchen on a Saturday afternoon.

'Hi.' I expected her to give some reason for being here, but instead she carried on telling Mum and Mike that she was born in Cape Town and had lived in Hong Kong and Dubai as well as London.

'What an interesting life! But it must have meant a lot of changing of schools,' Mum said.

'Oh no, Langtree's the first school I've been to. I never went, before. That's why it's all a bit weird.'

'Really?' Mum looked at me. 'You never told me that, Josh!'

I shuffled and mumbled.

'What about you, Kevin?' said Floss. 'Are you at the same school as Josh and me?'

'Nuh,' said Kevin. 'Don't live round here.' I noticed that he'd actually unplugged himself.

Floss was off. 'Oh, where do you live? What's your CD? Oh, *I* like them! Which track's your favourite? Have you heard —'

You'd have thought Kevin was the most fascinating person she'd ever met. I expected him to stare at the floor and answer with shrugs and Nuh and Duh, but instead he managed whole words. Once, even, he gave a funny little smile and it made him look almost *friendly.* I didn't know his face could do smiling. I sat next to Jennie and let her grip my finger and wondered if I could go back upstairs.

At last Floss stopped talking and rummaged in a rucksack she'd brought with her. 'I brought these for you, Josh. Thought you might like to borrow them.' She handed me two books and a brochure, on African wildlife and the South Kruger National Park. 'You can keep the brochure, but I want the books back.'

Mum leaned over to look. 'Oh, how kind of you! Isn't that lovely, Josh?'

I flicked through the brochure. There were some good pictures of lions and cheetahs in it – I could cut those out.

'Thanks,' I managed.

'Why don't you show Floss your Book of Cats, Josh?' said Mum.

I looked at her. *No* one was allowed to see my Book of Cats, outside of the family. Floss was bad enough, but *Kevin!* Didn't she realize? It was a bit much, being betrayed twice in one afternoon! – first Dad bringing Kevin when he'd said he wouldn't, and now this.

'No, no, I —' I blathered.

'Yes, why not bring it down here?' Mike joined in. 'I haven't seen it for a while.'

I suppose I could have done a Jamie strop and refused, but the main thing was to get rid of Floss before Dad came back, so I fetched it. She could have a quick look – she probably wouldn't be interested, anyway. It seemed pathetic, just a kid's collection of cutting-and-pasting and a few naff drawings.

I put it on the kitchen table and went back to Jennie.

'*Wow!*' went Floss. And she'd only got as far as the front cover.

Mum and Mike came over to look, too. So did Kevin.

'That's amazing! I love it!' Floss was going. 'All those eyes! Where did you find them all? How long have you been doing this?'

All those eyes gazed back at us. Cat eyes. Lion eyes. Tiger eyes. Cheetah eyes. Just the eyes, pairs of them staring from a black background. Amber eyes, golden eyes, burning eyes, eyes like headlamps, eyes like searchlights, eyes that looked as if they'd never blink or turn away.

Floss started flicking through the pages, looking at all the things I'd collected – pictures, articles I'd cut-and-pasted from the internet, facts and figures and stories and legends, photos of Mister the Magnificent and of Splodge. The way she gazed at my book, you'd have thought it was something special, something from a museum or a work of art.

'Wow!' she kept saying. Every time she turned a page, Mike went, 'Hey, look at that!' and Mum made surprised *mmm*ing noises. I felt like crawling into the cupboard under the sink, but they really were impressed, no messing, and I started to get a glowing feeling inside. It was a long time since I'd looked through the whole book.

'It's amazing,' said Floss.

I shrugged. 'I like facts. I collect them, that's all.'

'But these aren't just facts.' Floss turned another page. 'All this about myths and superstitions.'

'If you worked like this at school, Josh, you'd get A-star for everything,' Mike joked.

Then Floss came to the 'Tiger' poem. 'I nearly forgot!'

she said, and dug into her rucksack for a folded piece of paper. 'I copied this out for you. Mum and I read it at home a while back. You can have it for your book, if you like.'

It was called 'The Jaguar', by Ted Hughes. I read it quickly and didn't get all of it, but it was about a jaguar in a cage at the zoo, and people staring.

'That's really kind of you, Floss,' Mum said. 'Isn't it, Josh?'

'Yeah,' I said, and put the poem in my pocket to read properly later. I gave a defiant look at Kevin.

Floss was still turning the pages of my book when Dad and Jamie came back from the park. Jamie was teary-eyed and snivelly, but no one said anything about it. Of course Dad and Floss had to be introduced, and soon they were chatting, even though Jamie went silent at the sight of Floss. Then one thing led to another – without anyone even asking me, Floss was invited to stay for the bonfire and the supper. While she phoned home to tell her mum, I went a bit huffy. I mean, if I'd been *told* I could have a friend round, I'd have asked Noori. Instead I was lumbered with Floss, as well as Kevin. What would people at school say if they got to hear about this? Knowing Floss, she'd come straight out with it on Monday. 'When I was at Josh's house —' That kind of thing. How'd I explain that? About her coming round to give me a *poem?* Still, the good thing was that Floss could talk to Kevin, so I didn't have to.

It was starting to get dark now, so we all put on our coats and went out. Mike showed Jamie how to light a fire – paper first, then the kindling, the dried leaves and small twiggy bits we'd collected. The twigs would catch and hold the flame, then the heat would start to work at the bigger chunks of wood that would burn more slowly. Kevin joined in, too. Soon the flames were leaping, and flakes of charred paper drifted up into the dark. It wasn't the clear, frosty night I wanted, with the sky full of stars – instead, there was a cold wind snatching at us, and wispy bits of cloud covering the moon. You could still see stars, though – I picked out the Plough, and Orion the hunter, and Venus, which Dad said was the Evening Star. Our shadows fell ragged on the grass behind us, joined or separate – my shadow, Jamie's, Dad's, Kevin's.

Floss seemed quite at home. She told us about camp-fires on safari and how you could hear animals howling across the veldt.

'Fantastic,' said Dad. 'What an experience. You'll remember that your whole life.'

'I know,' said Floss. 'I do.'

I remembered standing out here when I was searching for Splodge, how mysterious it had felt, alone in the darkness. What if this was all we had for safety, this fire, and our supply of sticks? What if there was no bright kitchen window behind me, no central heating, no food in the fridge? What if these flames were the only barrier between us and the waiting lions? What if we had to go out and kill or be killed?

I looked at Jamie, wondering if he remembered what I'd told him, and whether it made any sense at all. He was crouching as close to the fire as he could, so that his face was lit up golden and flickering. I saw the whites of his eyes, and how young and little he was. The cold crept round behind me, whispering into my ears and down the back of my neck, while my front and face roasted. Mike was wearing Jennie in a sling, taking care she didn't get too hot, his big hand held up to protect her head.

I squatted next to Jamie. 'Remember,' I whispered to him. 'Lions are frightened of fire. We're not, and that means we can control them.'

He looked into the heart of the bonfire. I poked the burning papers with a stick, so that the flames flared up.

'The sausages must be nearly ready,' Mum told us.

Jennie started to whimper. I looked at her, and saw her little body straining in the sling, her mouth going square, ready to cry. I'd held her myself and knew how strong she was already, how she could kick and struggle and push. But how helpless, too. I thought of the dream – Jamie's dream, my dream – of Jennie in the lion's jaws, and I closed my eyes tight to make it go away. It was too horrible. The grown-ups would see, and would know –

Only it wasn't me, was it? It was Jamie. It was his dream, not mine.

Jennie began to wail. Out here, under the sky, her voice sounded as thin and frail as a fledgling's. On her own, she wouldn't stand a chance.

'Shush, shush!' Mike went. 'I think I'll take her in. Turn the oven off and put the beans on.'

I went across to stand by Dad. He put a hand on my shoulder and we stood like that for a few moments. I wanted to talk to him, like he'd said, only how could I, with Floss and Kevin here and the sausages nearly ready?

Mum had put glasses and cutlery on the table, but everyone wanted to eat by the fire. We wrapped the hot sausages in squares of kitchen towel and licked tomato sauce off our fingers, and we spooned the baked beans out of mugs.

'I don't know why, but food always tastes better outside,' Dad said.

Our meal was finished off with Mike's clementine cake, and hot chocolate. Soon Floss said she ought to be getting home. Dad offered to give her a lift, but Floss said it was only five minutes' walk.

'I've had a great time,' she said. 'Thanks so much!'

'We've enjoyed having you,' Mum told her. 'Come again.'

Although Floss said she was quite OK walking home on her own, Dad wasn't having it. He and I went with her. Her house was bigger than ours, with its own drive and a big 4x4 parked there. Floss's mum was tall and friendly, with blonde hair like Floss's only cut very short, and the same loud, confident voice. 'So you're Josh! I've heard lots about you.' She must have wanted the whole street to hear. 'Come round after school one day. Any time.'

Dad and I said goodbye and turned for home.

'It's good you've made a new friend,' Dad said.

It seemed too late now to say that Floss wasn't exactly my friend. Maybe she *was*. Better than Brody, anyway. Brody and I had been friends since I'd first started at St Luke's – Noori had joined the class later – and yesterday's argument lurked unhappily in my mind. But that was his fault, not mine.

'Dad,' I began, not sure what to say next. 'You know about Jamie? All this weird stuff?'

Jamie had begged me not to tell, not to tell anyone. If I didn't mention the lion dream, though, the nightmare, I'd have kept my promise.

'Mm?' Dad was listening, waiting.

'Jamie's jealous of the baby. Jealous of Jennie.'

There, it was out now. Dad would know what to do. I looked at him sideways. He said nothing at all while we walked past the newsagent's, the fish-and-chip shop, the Indian restaurant with its waft of music and spices and chatter. Then he said, 'Do you remember when Splodge was a tiny kitten, eight weeks old? When we first brought him home?'

'Yes, course,' I said. 'I've got photos.' What was he on about?

'Do you remember Mister? How he behaved? He'd been an only cat up till then – now suddenly there was this little stranger in the house, Splodge. And we were all making a great fuss of the kitten.'

Yes, I remembered. 'Mister had a huge sulk! He stayed out at night and wouldn't come when we called him. He only came in for meals and went out again as soon as he'd eaten. He used to give us such a *look*. And Splodge used to leap and pounce on him, and Mister hissed and growled and got really fed up with him.'

'It was so difficult for a while,' Dad said, 'that I wondered whether we'd made a mistake getting Splodge, because it didn't seem fair to Mister. I mean, we couldn't *explain* to Mister that we still loved him just as much. Of course we did. And before long they were the best of friends. Remember how they'd lie in front of the fire together, licking each other's fur? How they used to curl up and sleep? How they played together with their ping-pong ball?'

I nodded. 'And when Mister had to be put to sleep, Splodge was upset for days. He kept looking for Mister all

The Greeks believed that the god Zeus placed the figure of a gigantic lion in the sky with the rest of the stars. The Zodiac Leo is named after this lion constellation.

This Lion might be the one Hercules fought. Hercules had twelve tasks to do, and one was to kill a ferocious lion. It was called the Nemean Lion and it killed anyone who went near it. It was bigger and stronger than any other lion, but what made it practically impossible to kill was that its skin couldn't be injured by metal, stone or wood. So ordinary weapons were useless.

---

over the house and all over the garden. Kept miaowing for him.'

'Change,' said Dad. 'That's what's difficult.'

I looked at him.

'Lots of people don't like change,' he said. 'Grown-ups as well as children. Animals as well as humans. We like what we know, and it upsets us when we have to get used to something different, especially if we haven't chosen it. You and Jamie have had to face a lot of changes, haven't you? The Kim and Kevin situation, as well. Perhaps it's all been a bit too much.'

Kevin? I ignored that, and said, 'Will Jamie be all right, then?'

'I'm sure he will,' Dad said. 'It may take time, but I'm sure he will. D'you know who's going to be the biggest help to him?'

I shrugged. 'The psychologist?'

Dad put his arm round my shoulders and pulled me close. 'You are. His big brother. I know how much you're helping him through this. I'm proud of you. And so's Mum, because you're being such a good big brother to Jennie as well.'

I felt funny and squirmy, the way I always do when Dad talks like that. Besides, it wasn't *true*. But it made me decide that I'd try to be a better brother, to both of them.

We were nearly home now. 'I wonder if that bonfire's still burning?' Dad said. 'And if there's any of that cake left?'

22

ASHES

It's always like this, every time I decide I'm going to be better, or nicer, or try harder at school, or whatever. Something always turns up to make me fail. P'raps it's a kind of test – *OK, let's see how you handle this. Let's see how you shape up.*

Well, if this was a test, I failed big time. Mind you, only a saint could have passed, and then only on a good day.

I don't know what Dad said to Jamie when they went to the park, or what Jamie said back. Jamie seemed excited, out by the bonfire, and when we were eating – happier than I'd seen him for ages. But later, after Dad and Kevin had gone, he went quiet again. Sunday morning, I couldn't get a word out of him. He's often like this after we've seen Dad.

I woke up early, and read for about half an hour before Jamie even moved. Then I noticed that he was lying in bed with his eyes open.

'Hi, Jame,' I said.

He wouldn't even look at me. Slowly, he rubbed his eyes and propped himself up.

'Open the curtains if you want,' I said.

Nothing.

I got out of bed, and opened the curtains myself. Jamie just lay there, staring at nothing. The bonfire, Dad coming, the private talk – none of it might have happened, for all the difference in Jamie.

I didn't feel like going back to bed. Mike quite often works on Saturdays, so Sunday's his only chance of a lie-in. Usually Jennie wakes up early, but Mum feeds her and Mike goes down to make tea, and sometimes they go back to sleep again, unless Jennie won't settle. If Jamie or I get up early, we're supposed to be quiet till at least eight o'clock.

While I was getting dressed, I felt the crackle of paper in my jeans pocket and took out a folded page. It was that poem Floss had given me, the one about the jaguar. I read it properly now, and liked it. It had this really good bit about the jaguar prowling up and down in his cage, with his eyes boring into the dark like drills. I could see that, and I already had just the right picture of a jaguar, so I decided to copy and print the poem and stick it in my Book of Cats.

When I'd done the print-out, I looked round for my book. It was usually on the desk, but the computer and printer now took up nearly all the space. Not there. Course, I took it downstairs last night, when Mum and Mike made me show it to Floss. Hadn't I brought it back up? No, can't have. I went down to the kitchen, but the table had been cleared. Checked the worktop – not there either. Looked in the lounge.

Jamie was still asleep, hunched away from me, when I went back to our room. I looked everywhere – under the desk, in all the drawers, under both beds, even in the wardrobe. No sign. Down again to double-check all the places I'd already searched. I began to think Floss must have stolen it, put it in her rucksack, and taken it home. I didn't really think Floss would do that, but couldn't come up with anything better.

I was working myself up into a real fume, ready to march straight round to her house and demand my book back. Then I remembered something.

Last night, when Dad was ready to go home, he called for Jamie to say goodbye. Mum and Mike thought Jamie was upstairs in our room, but he wasn't. I was the one who noticed the back door wasn't quite closed. When I opened it wide and looked out, there was Jamie, by himself, standing by the remains of the fire – no coat on, no hat or gloves.

'What you doing?' I called. 'Come on in – Dad's going now.'

He must have heard me, but he didn't answer, or turn round.

'Jamie?' I called, starting to shiver. 'Come on – I'm not standing here all night!'

He came in then, and Mike said, 'Jamie? What were you *doing?*'

And Jamie peered at him like someone groping through a fog, and said, 'Just making sure.'

'Making sure the fire's safe? Don't worry,' said Mike, 'I was going to do that, when I lock up.'

Dad kissed and hugged us both, and said he'd be back on Monday, and Jamie and I went up to bed.

No!

He wouldn't – he couldn't have . . .

My hands were shaking so much I could hardly unlock the back door. I went across the wet grass in my slippers to the blackened patch where the bonfire had been. It was just a pile of ashes and crumbly twigs, with charred bits of paper the flames had missed. I poked at the ashes with a stick, turned over a curl of paper, and saw something startling, something familiar –

An eye, a single amber lion eye, wise and unblinking, stared up from a triangle of torn black paper.

An eye from the cover of my Book of Cats.

Something had got inside my chest, pushing against my ribs, pressing up to my throat. I could hardly breathe. I poked and twisted, saw fragments of my own handwriting, a corner of a photo, bits of printing. I lifted a handful of ashes and let them filter through my fingers, leaving me with scraps and tatters of paper, brown and flaky-thin. There was still a little warmth left at the heart of the fire.

The whole book, not just the cover.

Gone.

Destroyed.

That's what Jamie had been doing, out here on his own last night.

A choking sound burst out of me. He couldn't have – not *all* of it, every page! I looked in the dustbin, just in case he'd chucked some of it in there. Inside, I saw the back cover, made of thick card, with its spiral binding twanging away from it, bent and spoiled when the pages had been ripped out. The only bit that wouldn't burn. For some reason that made me even more furious. He'd *planned* this, thought about it!

I ran inside, startling Splodge who was waiting by his food bowl in the kitchen. I thundered up the stairs, not caring if I woke the whole house.

'Jamie!' I yelled. 'JAMIE!'

He was still in bed, curled up like a dormouse. I bounded across the room and hauled the duvet off him.

'Why?' I shouted. 'Why did you do it?'

If he'd been asleep, he was certainly wide awake now. He wriggled back against the headboard, making himself as small as he could. His eyes, bright and worried, made me think of a frightened little animal. A squirrel or a shrew, quivering with fright.

I was too angry to care. I wanted to hit him, hurt him, make him pay. 'Why? Come on – I know you did it!' I was kneeling on his bed, pushing my face close to his. I saw tears well up in his eyes, then spill over, big and splashy.

'That's right, start blubbing! Go all pathetic! You did it, didn't you? Last night. I know you did, you burned my book – come on, tell me WHY!'

He started to snivel. 'You told me! You told me to!'

'I did not! Don't try to blame me!'

'You did!' he whimpered. 'And I tore up Leo as well and threw the pieces on the fire –'

'What, your pathetic paper mask? You think that makes it OK?' I bunched the duvet in my hands, gripped and twisted it. 'I hate you, Jamie, I swear I do —'

Suddenly Mum was in the room in a flurry of blue

dressing-gown. 'What on earth's going on? What's the matter?'

'*He's* the matter! He – he —' Tears blurred my eyes, my voice gave way, a big sob pushed at my throat. 'He burned my Book of Cats! Tore it up and chucked it on the fire! Like it was – like it was rubbish —'

'No! Jamie wouldn't do that —'

'He *did!* Go and see for yourself if you don't believe me! I'll never forgive him for that, ever!' I swiped at my eyes with the back of my hand and stood up, turning my face to the window. All I could think of was my book, my beautiful book. My work of art, Mum had called it last night. My book that I loved. My project, just for me. My special book that I'd worked at for months – the pictures I'd cut out and collected, cuttings from newspapers and magazines, the photos of Mister and Splodge, things that could never be replaced.

Mum sat on Jamie's bed. 'Did you do it, Jamie?' she asked, very serious. I didn't even look round, just stared out of the window at the paper-boy's bike leaning against a lamp-post. Jamie snivelled and sniffed, didn't answer, but he must have nodded, because Mum went, 'Oh, Jamie! *Why?* Josh's lovely book!' When I turned, she was cuddling him – cuddling *him!* – and rocking him like a baby, and he was gulping and sobbing and wiping his runny nose on his pyjama sleeve.

'That's right!' I shouted. 'Let him get away with it, sweet little Jamiekins! What if I'd ruined something of *his,* done it on purpose, then what? I'm sick of this! I'm not sharing a room with him any more – I hate him!'

In the background Jennie started to cry, and Mike brought her in to see what all the yelling was about. For a confused few minutes it seemed we were *all* crying, except Mike, and even he looked pretty upset. He stayed with Jamie while Mum and I went down to the garden to examine the evidence.

'Oh, dear, and I thought last night went so well!' She was shivering, cuddling herself into her dressing-gown. 'Joshie, I know you're upset – your beautiful book! It was an awful, awful thing for Jamie to do, and he'll have to realise that. This thing of his about Leo and lions! I wish I understood it.' She was talking in the sad, worried voice she used so often nowadays, the small defeated voice. 'D'you know, I nearly said something to you last night, when I saw your front cover with the eyes on it. All those eyes staring. I was going to say perhaps you should put it away in your desk, after all this business with masks and nightmares. Only with Floss and Kevin and Dad here and the bonfire, I forgot.'

'Right, so it's my fault?' I fired back.

Mum tried to hug me, but I wriggled away. 'No, no, of course not!' she said. 'But Jamie's very disturbed, and we've all got to try to help him. I know it's hard for you, but he needs you, Joshie. We all do. Come on, it's cold – let's go in and do something about breakfast. Then I'm going to phone your dad and tell him what's happened, and I'm going to try to have a good talk with Jamie. Have you got any plans for today? Do you want to see if Brody can come round, or Noori? Or both of them?'

I mumbled a No. I hadn't told Mum about the fight with Brody and I didn't want to think about that now. Whenever I was at home with nothing particular to do, I went back to my Book of Cats. Without it, I felt sick and hollow.

We went in, and Mike came down to make porridge while Mum went up to Jennie. I didn't want to eat breakfast with Jamie, and didn't see how he could begin to put things right. Tears would be useless. Sorry would be useless. The only thing that wouldn't be useless was to give me back my Book of Cats. Undo what he'd done.

Peaceful Sunday morning, not. But that was only the beginning.

23
Gone

That afternoon, Jamie disappeared.

Slipped out of the house when none of us was looking.

Course, we didn't realise at first – we thought he was hiding. We called for him, we searched and searched again, we looked in every cupboard and under the beds and in the wardrobes and out in the garden and in Mike's van.

Mike was the first to say what we were all thinking. 'He must have gone out.'

'Out?' shrieked Mum. 'Out where? On his own? Without telling us?'

She flung open the front door and ran out into the street, and stood gazing one way and then the other. Mike and I followed.

'No need to panic,' Mike told her. 'He'll be back in a minute. Maybe he's gone round to Arran's, or gone to the newsagent's. You go in – I'll scout round and see if I can find him. No – we can't *all* go – Liz, you stay here with

Jennie and Josh. Most likely he'll turn up while I'm gone.'

Course, it's not as if Jamie never goes out of the house on his own – he is nine, after all. He often goes to Arran's or round to the shops. But he was already in a state today, and – and –

And I'd told him I hated him. Told him I'd never forgive him.

In a hurry, I searched everywhere all over again, even in places like the washing-basket and in the big drawers under Mum and Mike's bed where sheets and duvet covers are kept, and Mum phoned Arran's mum to see if he'd gone round there. 'No? Just checking. See you tomorrow, then. No, he'll turn up right as rain, don't worry.'

But she didn't fool me. When she put the phone down, she was starting to cry, and trying to pretend she wasn't.

'Do you think he might try to get to Dad's?' she asked me, then answered her own question. 'But how could he? He's only been there once, and by car – he wouldn't know how – still, maybe – *When* did he go, Josh?' She looked wild and panicky. 'He's hardly been out of my sight all day. What time, exactly?'

I worked out that he must have been gone about twenty-five minutes. Mum had been changing Jennie's nappy, and Mike was clearing up after lunch, and I was gloomily watching TV downstairs. I'd heard Jamie come down the stairs, and he might even have come into the front room, but because I was in such a strop with him I hadn't turned round from the screen. Now, thinking, I went cold and prickly, goose-pimples shivering all over my skin and inside as well. Jamie had asked me, hadn't he, about running away from home? About money, and where I'd go?

I ran up to our room and opened the smallest desk drawer, where my Christmas money was in an envelope, waiting till I got the chance to buy my binoculars.

Where my Christmas money *had* been in an envelope.

There was nothing there now.

A shiver trickled all the way down my back, like ice melting. What did this mean? Jamie hadn't just gone round the corner, that was for sure. He hadn't gone to see Arran. He'd run away from home.

I went down and told Mum. She listened, pale and still.

'Right, that's it. I'm phoning the police.'

She dialled 999, which had always seemed to be an exciting thing to do, only now it felt like acting out some *Crimewatch* thing. Awful pictures started playing themselves in my head. I thought of Jamie's photo in the newspapers, people searching through parks and waste ground. I thought of crime scenes barricaded off with police tape. I thought of other children who'd gone missing and been found dead in woods. And with a horrible lurch of dread, I remembered that man who offered me a lift at the Underground station. I knew better than to get into a car with a stranger, but Jamie was younger – what if he was lost, and alone, and frightened, and met a stranger who offered to help him?

Mum phoned Dad as well, then she started to cry – without tears, just great sobs that heaved themselves out of her. She got up, went to the front door, came back and snatched a tissue out of her bag.

'I can't just sit here!' she kept muttering. 'Not while Jamie's – Why did we let him down? How did we get it so wrong? Where would he go, Josh? To Arran's – to some other friend? To Gran and Grandad Bryce, or to Nan's? – I'll phone them – no, I don't want to worry them, not till —'

I didn't know what to do, so I went to Jennie for comfort, because she was the only person not involved in this. She was just starting to smile, and she kept gazing into my face and then cooing and shaking her fists in delight. Usually Mum would smile and coo back, but now she didn't even notice. I lifted Jennie out of the crib and held her, smelled her sweet baby warmth, felt how plump and strong she was, how alive, how eager to live. How she completed our family. But now there was a Jamie-sized gap in the middle. Nothing would feel right until he was back. I'd lied when I said I hated him – I knew that. I'd lied when I said I'd never forgive him. He's my brother, my Jamie, and without him I wouldn't be the same Josh. It would be like having an arm or a leg cut off.

Mum and I both jumped when we heard Mike's key in the lock. We all sagged with disappointment – Mike because he hoped Jamie would have turned up, and us because we hoped Mike had found him. Mum told him about the money, and the police, and he said he was going to knock at all the houses in the street.

I ran after him. I had to do *something*. The police would come and start taking statements and alerting all the patrol cars like they do on TV dramas. Once all that started, I could only imagine the kinds of ending I didn't want to think about.

It was grey and cold and a bit drizzly, not the sort of day that would make you want to hang around outside if you didn't have to. There was a skip in the road four houses down from ours, the kind people hire when they're having a big clear-out, and I pulled myself up and had a good look, just in case Jamie had thought of hiding inside. Mike was talking to Mrs Al-Safadi at the next door along. Of course he was having to give a detailed explanation, and it'd take him ages if he did that at every door. Jamie wasn't in the skip, so I went on past, trying to think what I'd do if I was him. I concentrated hard, closing my eyes, willing myself into his head. Where would I go? What would I do?

Jamie's head was a very muddly place to go, that was the problem. Full of eyes and shadows and flames and bad feelings. Only I couldn't tell which bad feelings were Jamie's and which were mine.

This was my fault, wasn't it? How could it not be? I'd told him I hated him, told him I'd never forgive him . . .

But I didn't mean it. Really didn't mean it.

'Jamie!' I thought, so hard that I felt all my muscles clench. 'Come home. Please come home. I didn't mean what I said. Everything's all right as long as you come home.'

I'd reached the end of Lansdowne Avenue where it joined the High Street. Although I knew I shouldn't go on without telling Mike, so that he didn't think I'd wandered off as well, I couldn't resist going just a bit further. To the bus stop, then to the next corner. All the time, I was scanning both sides of the street – the shop doorways, the pub with its brightly-lit windows, an alleyway with bin-bags piled up. Then a movement caught my eye. There! In the narrow passageway – just a glimpse of something that had dodged out of sight. Had I imagined it? Or had there been a small hunched figure, a frightened face, eyes staring at me across the street?

'Jamie!' I yelled, and dashed into the road.

Something rocketed into me and lifted me off my feet and slammed me down in the gutter. I heard a skid and screech and clash of metal. The breath was knocked out of me so hard that I heard myself wheezing for air. There was a sick, awful pain in my ankle that made me reel and gasp. I wondered if I was dead, or would be dead soon.

A voice shouted from very far away. Hands were clutching at me, faces looming. My head was in the road and I had a beetle's-eye view of the sky and the tall buildings and the faces that crowded over me. I seemed to be breathing, though it felt as if I'd only just learned how.

I saw a mouth moving. 'OK, I think he's OK —'

'No, don't move him —'

'Jamie,' I gasped, as soon as I'd got enough air to speak. 'My brother. He's —'

But I couldn't see. A thick, clotty blackness came between me and the faces. All of me felt unbelievably limp and heavy, and I was pulled down into the darkness.

24
MISTER

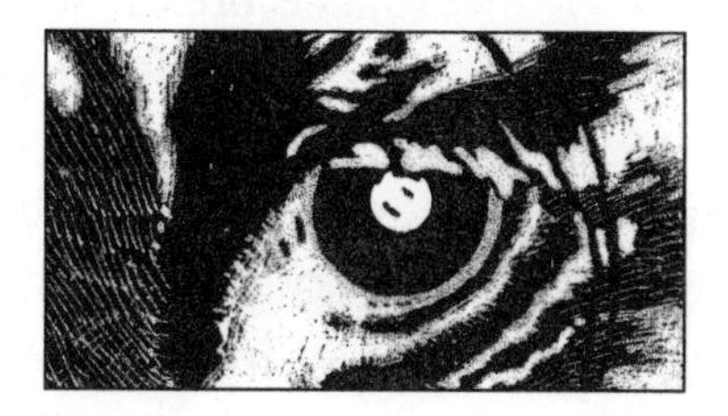

Things got confusing after that. I was lying on a bed, and a man was sitting by me, and my eyes seemed to have swivelled out of control.

'You're in an ambulance,' the man said, and his face loomed towards me like a fish in a glass tank, then swam away again. 'You're OK. You're being looked after. You were hit by a motor-bike, do you remember?'

A bit later a voice in the darkness asked what my name was, and I heard myself answering.

Then I seemed to have been asleep for a very long time. I woke up warm and comfortable and still sleepy. There was a big heaviness on my leg that stopped me from moving.

It was nice here, so I slept some more. Next I slid into one of those dreams that seems so clear and detailed, it feels like a story – a story you're making up for yourself by dreaming it, only it goes off in peculiar directions. This one was about Mister, dear old Mister the Magnificent. I'd often had Mister dreams before. In my Book of Cats

I'd stuck a list of cat superstitions, and one of them said that if you dream about a tabby cat it means you're going to have good luck. But if I dreamed a Mister dream, I just thought it meant I'd dreamed about Mister. And now that he was dead, I sometimes dreamed about Splodge instead.

But this was definitely Mister. In the dream, I was running along a street, a long street of houses and dustbins and parked cars, a street that never seemed to end. I was out of breath, panting, bent double, but I had to go on. I stopped dead when I saw Mister, sitting on a low brick wall. He was looking at me, and I knew he'd been waiting. He knew I'd come that way.

I stared into his big green eyes and they gazed back at me with all their cat wisdom. He blinked slowly, holding my eyes with his. Although he didn't speak out loud, I heard quite clearly what he said.

'Cat is cat is cat. Cat isn't what humans make of us. Cat is cat and always cat. Cat is cat, now and for all time.'

Then he turned and jumped down from the wall, and I knew he meant me to follow. We were in an alleyway between tall buildings, where Mister weaved between piles of bin-bags and I had to trip and stumble over them. It was dark in the alley, with no daylight getting in, but I had the sense of sunshine far ahead. At last we emerged from the tunnel and were standing on a grass plain, fields and meadows as far as I could see. I squinted into dazzling sun.

I recognised this place. The wildlife park, and I was

standing in front of the lion enclosure. There was no fence now, no glass panel, but I saw the group of lions on their grassy knoll – the male, the female, the two cubs, just like last time.

Jamie was standing next to me. 'Where've you been?' he said. 'I've been waiting ages.'

We stood together as the male lion paced towards us. I felt Jamie tremble, but neither of us could move, and anyway there was nowhere to hide. Mister stayed next to us, completely still. I hadn't noticed till now, but he'd grown and grown to the size of a lion, so that without bending down I stood with my hand on his back, buried in his thick warm fur. The lion walked slackly on padded paws, his tail slung low, his mane dense and rough. I could smell the hot wildness of him, see the sun reflected in his eyes.

A few metres away, he stopped. Lifted his head. Stared.

Mister didn't move. None of us did. They stood gazing at each other, cat to cat.

Then the lion gave a sighing sound, and lay down on the grass. He curled one front paw round and began licking it, like Mister did when he washed himself.

'See, Jamie,' I said, or maybe it was Mister who spoke. 'He's not evil or vicious. He's a cat, doing cat things. He eats and he sleeps, he washes himself and he thinks his cat thoughts. Come on, let's go home now.'

'Can we?' said Jamie. 'I'm tired.'

We turned to walk away, but found ourselves instead on the top deck of a bus with no roof. Bright lights shone into my face. I seemed to be lying in bed, but I was on wheels and there was a ceiling above me and walls each side and I had to grab the sides of the bed or I'd fall off.

'You're all right, Josh,' said a woman's voice. 'We're taking you to the ward.'

Ward? What ward? Where was I?

'Jamie!' I said. 'I've lost him again —' But it felt like trying to talk underwater. My words came out all slurred and burbled, so I gave up. We were going round corners, through swing doors, coming to a stop. I don't think I woke up properly till I'd been unloaded on to a proper bed and wedged into a sitting-up position, with lots of pillows. My eyes snapped open when I saw all the people sitting or standing round me. Mum. Dad. Mike, with Jennie.

And Jamie. Jamie, looking pale, eyes round and frightened, but definitely Jamie.

'What's going on?' I asked blearily.

'If you were a cat,' Dad said, 'you'd have used up one of your nine lives.'

25
JOSH'S BOOK

Considering I'd dived off the pavement in front of a motor-bike, I was lucky. I was concussed and bruised all over. I'd chipped the bone in my leg just above the ankle, and my leg would be in plaster for six weeks. They were keeping me in hospital for a couple of nights. The motor-cyclist had swerved drastically and almost wrapped his bike round a lamppost, but had no worse injury than a few scratches to his metalwork and a bad shock.

'Honestly, Josh,' Mum said, 'all the worrying I did about Jamie crossing roads without looking, and it was you who ran out in front of a bike!'

'I saw Jamie,' I remembered. 'Jamie, in an alleyway.'

'No, it couldn't have been. Jamie wasn't there.'

But Jamie was back, and that was the important thing. Police had been looking for him, and a WPC had come to our house to say I'd been carted off in an ambulance – 'I don't want another day like that, *ever*,' Mum said with a shudder.

Through that evening, we had bits and scraps of

conversation. I seemed to dip in and out of it, floating to the surface for a quick snatch, then drifting under again. Most of the time Mum was there, and sometimes Mike, and sometimes Dad, and even Kevin. And Jamie.

Finally, when everyone in the ward was settling down for sleep and the lights turned dim, I was wide awake. Dad was still with me, but visiting hours were officially over and the nurses were about to shoo him away.

'When did Jamie come back?' I asked him blearily.

'Must have been about the time you were in the ambulance. The odd thing was,' Dad told me, 'it was Kevin who guessed.'

'Guessed?'

'Where Jamie was most likely to go.'

Dad explained that when Mum had phoned, he was over at Kim's house doing some plastering. Kevin was there, and wanted to come with him. Two police were in our kitchen by then, and everyone sat round the table trying to think where Jamie was most likely to go. Gran and Grandad Bryce's, Dad thought. Nan's, at Woodford, was Mum's idea. 'A friend's house, from school?' the woman policeman asked, and wrote down names. Then Kevin came out with, 'I bet he's gone to that zoo place. That place you went to at New Year.'

'What, the Cotswold Wildlife Park?' Dad said. 'No, there's no way he could do that. It's miles out in the country. No buses or trains go there.'

Mum asked Kevin why he'd thought of that, but Kevin shrugged and said, 'Just an idea.'

But Kevin's guess was closer than anyone else's. How hadn't I guessed? Jamie was trying to get to London Zoo. By now his description had been circulated and police were out looking for him in patrol cars. We'd been to the Zoo three years ago and Jamie knew it was in Regent's Park, so he'd bought an Underground ticket and got on the Metropolitan line as far as King's Cross. Here he got himself confused, and didn't know where to go next (I could have told him, you want Camden Town for the Zoo, couple of stops on the Northern line), and he was standing in a dither when a kind woman saw him on his own and thought he might be in trouble. When she asked where his mum and dad were, he burst into tears and ran off towards the Hammersmith and City line. The woman was concerned and called the police on her mobile, just in case Jamie was a Missing Person. Which he was, by then. Small boy on his own, thick brown hair, brown eyes, blue jeans, navy anorak, may be frightened or upset. A policeman spotted him at Baker Street Underground.

I stayed in hospital for two more nights. I was kept busy with meals and washing, exercises and injections and visitors, but there was also plenty of time for thinking. And I saw a weird Jamie-logic in everything he'd done.

The lion had scared him by looking at him, but it was really his own thoughts that frightened him. I'd tried to help by saying that flames would send the lion away, the lion of his dreams, but that backfired on me when Jamie did the obvious thing – to him, anyway – and burned my book, with its staring cats' eyes. Now the Zoo.

'Why the Zoo, Jame?' I asked, next time he visited.

'See a lion. See if it worked,' he said, in an *isn't-it-obvious* kind of way. 'See if I could just look at it, and then look at monkeys and giraffes.' He was more interested in the Chelsea magazine he'd brought me.

He'd been to the child psychologist that afternoon,

with Mum and Dad. It didn't sound nearly as serious as I'd expected – he'd drawn pictures and played games, that was all, and he was going again next week. But the running away, and my accident, seemed to have shocked him back into himself. He was much more like my brother Jamie. I was sent home from hospital and had the rest of the week off school, and Jamie and I played chess and Playstation and watched TV in the afternoons when he came in.

On Thursday, Noori and Brody came round, with a big get-well card signed by everyone in the form. Brody said he was sorry for stirring things up and I said I was sorry for starting the fight, and they both tried out my crutches. Floss turned up as well, bringing me a book called *The Dreamfighter,* and said, 'Hey! Let's play standing-long-jump,' which turned out to be a game even I could join in. What you do is, you make a start line – we used the edge of the rug – and each player in turn takes one swing with the crutches from a standing start, and you mark carefully where the heel of their back foot lands. Noori had just set a new record when Mum heard the laughing and cheering and came to tell me that people recovering from concussion shouldn't be having quite so much fun. Mike was home from work by then, and he started showing us how to juggle with three apples. Brody was best, and got so keen on it that we couldn't make him stop. So Mike got pencil and paper and drew a cartoon of Brody juggling, with a look of panic on his face, and ten arms whizzing out so that he looked like a helicopter. Brody had seen Mike's cartoons before, but Floss and Noori hadn't, and they wanted Mike to draw them too. They all ended up staying for Mike's home-made pizza and ice-cream, and it was as good as a party. Jamie was doing his funny laugh, his *hic-hic-a-hic-a-hicca-hic,* and I knew we were getting him back.

And when I went up to bed, and saw a cat-shaped purring hump under Jamie's duvet that Mum would never allow if she found out, I knew that Splodge knew, too.

Jamie had given back my Christmas money, and on our next weekend in High Wycombe Dad took us to a big department store. Kevin, too. By now I could reach turbo speed on my crutches, and people scattered out of my way and held doors open and smiled. I think Jamie and Kevin were a little bit envious. After I'd chosen my binoculars (Viking 8x25, compact, waterproof), Jamie wanted to buy me a new notebook to make up for the one he'd burned. I think it was really Dad's idea, not Jamie's, but Jamie was happy to go along with it.

We stood and looked at the shelves and all the books on display – lots of them girly and sparkly, some of them plain, some with photos or stripes or logos.

'You can have whatever one you want,' Jamie told me.

We spent a long time looking. Eventually I chose a sketchpad, so that I could do a collage on the cover, like last time. Course, it was only an empty book – it wouldn't make up for all that was lost. But I couldn't help feeling a tingle of excitement when I thought about the smooth, grainy sheets waiting to be filled, and how special it would be when I'd made it mine. I thought about all the things I didn't know yet that would find their way into those pages.

26
BEING ALIVE

In Chinese myths, lions aren't fierce or dangerous. Instead they chase away evil spirits and bring good luck.
Fancy-dress lions help to celebrate happy occasions and new beginnings, like weddings, the opening of shops, the Chinese New Year and other new beginnings.

Equinox. We'd reached the Spring equinox, which Dad said was one of the year's marker-posts – the day when night and day are the same length, and the days are going to stretch out now into summer.

For Jennie, *every*thing was a marker-post as the year went round. Everything was a first. She was three months old now, and could smile and make little exclaiming or chuckling noises. She was starting to lift her head and turn it to look at things. She could hold her plastic duck for a few moments. She could grab hold of one of her feet, and we thought she knew it belonged to her. Next thing, according to Mum's book, she'd start trying to sit up, to get a different view of the world. Most evenings now, after she'd had her bath, Jamie read her a story. Of course she didn't understand, but she seemed to like Jamie talking to her and helping to put her to bed. Sometimes I did the reading, because Jamie still liked having a story read to him. And sometimes Mum or Mike read to all three of us.

Every afternoon, as soon as I got home from school, I spent some time with Jennie. I loved watching her notice things, wondering what she thought. It fascinated me that she was Jennie, she was herself and the self she would grow into (where had she come from? Where was she going?), but she was also a fully-programmed human being. Somewhere inside her, ready, was all this instinct that had been instinct for as long as humans were humans. Instinct would tell her when it was time to crawl, when to push herself up to her feet, when to trust and when to be frightened, how to listen and learn and try new things. And she already knew how to make people love her and look after her.

When I held her, I thought of everything she'd have to do as she got older – all the fun and the hurts and the frustrations and the wonder, the falling ill and the getting better, the making friends and enemies, the breaking and the mending. It seemed too much for one small baby to have to face. But when I said this to Mum, or at least something like it, she laughed. 'But that's what being alive is made of, Joshie. No one has to live their whole life all at once. It'll wait till she's ready.'

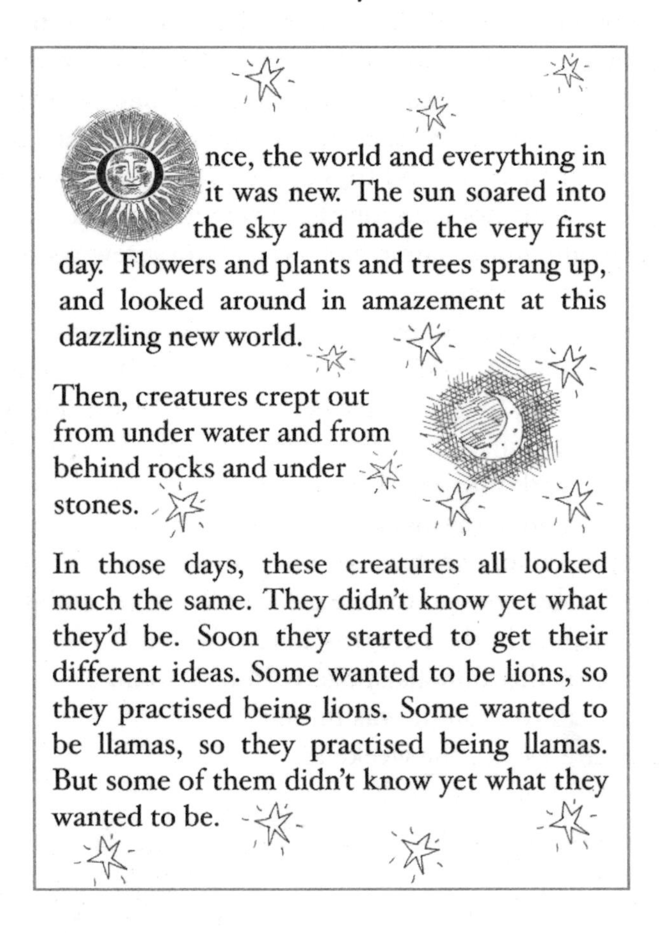

Once, the world and everything in it was new. The sun soared into the sky and made the very first day. Flowers and plants and trees sprang up, and looked around in amazement at this dazzling new world.

Then, creatures crept out from under water and from behind rocks and under stones.

In those days, these creatures all looked much the same. They didn't know yet what they'd be. Soon they started to get their different ideas. Some wanted to be lions, so they practised being lions. Some wanted to be llamas, so they practised being llamas. But some of them didn't know yet what they wanted to be.

My leg was out of plaster now and I'd had to give the crutches back, which was a pity, really – I'd got used to them. A scar above my ankle was all that was left from my accident. I'd even be doing PE again soon.

After his first visit to the child psychologist, Jamie went a few more times. Once Mike and Mum went without Jamie, and twice Dad took Jamie, and once *I* went. It wasn't nearly as interesting as I'd expected. The psychologist was only an ordinary person, a woman with red curly hair and shiny shoes and a silver dolphin brooch on her jacket. Instead of couches and bright lights and electrodes and diagrams of the brain, her consulting room was full of cushions and toys and books. We just talked a bit, then went home. Soon there was no need for any of us to go any more. Jamie had liked the first few visits, but now he was bored.

Because Jamie had been trying to get to London Zoo to look at the lions, Dad took us back to the Wildlife Park. We enjoyed it, but the lions weren't doing much this time. I didn't tell Dad, but I'd far rather go to the South Kruger National Park and see them in the wild. Jamie looked at the lions and went back a second time to see if they'd woken up, but he was more interested in the Giant Tortoises, big enough to ride on, and the Red Pandas who were sleeping in their trees – 'Like ripe plums,' Dad said.

None of the animals spoke to Jamie, or if they did he didn't seem to think it was important.

Kev and I spent the weekend after the Equinox with Dad – digging, mainly. We were making a pond in Dad's back garden. It took an awful lot of digging, and even when the hole looked deep enough for a small pond, Dad said he wanted it twice the size. We dug and we dug and we dug some more, getting filthy and tired. You wouldn't believe how much soil you dig out when you start making even a middling-sized hole. We collected bucket-loads of stones, and we carted the soil away in barrows and piled it in one corner, for Dad to use on the garden. I imagined a pond with reed-fringed edges, damselflies hovering over the water, and newts and frogs poking their heads out. Dad said he couldn't think of anything better than turning a patch of grass into such a rich habitat. 'They'll all find their way here, the damselflies and the amphibians,' he said, 'if we make it their kind of place.'

We didn't spend *all* weekend digging. It was Kevin's birthday on the Sunday and Kim took him paintballing with his friends. Jamie and I went too. We're OK, Kev and Jamie and me. Kevin's shy, Dad says, and that can look like unfriendliness at first. But he's sort of family. We're three Js and a K, and we're used to that now.

I wrote about the pond in my new notebook, leaving space for before-and-after photos. I was going to do the *Edwardian Lady* thing, and note down the dates – first dragonfly, first frog, first bird or hedgehog drinking pond water.

This book had turned out differently from the first one. The night we bought it, I started collaging the cover. Even though Jamie hadn't had any more dreams about staring cats, it didn't seem a good idea to do the eyes this time. I'd do habitats.

Dad was always giving me *National Geographic* magazines, so it wasn't hard to find forests and drinking-holes and desert and savannah and scrub. I began searching for letters to cut out for the title, Book of Cats, but then I stopped and looked at what I'd got.

There was no point trying to re-make the book I'd made before. I had a special liking for the cat family and probably always would, but maybe I should move on now. This book didn't know what it wanted to be, yet. After all, there was the rest of the animal kingdom, not to mention the world, the solar system, the universe, infinity. And I only had one life to discover it all.

So I called it Josh's Book of Everything.

ACKNOWLEDGEMENTS

The poem Floss gives Josh is 'The Jaguar' by Ted Hughes, first published in *Hawk in the Rain,* 1957. Ted Hughes is also the author of *The Dreamfighter* (Faber, 2003); the book Floss lends Josh after his accident. The creation story Josh writes in his new notebook on page 176 is his version of the beginning of *How the Whale Became,* the first section of *The Dreamfighter.*

In the interests of accuracy (at the time of writing), the Asian lioness at the Cotswold Wildlife Park last gave birth to cubs in 1999. These lions are part of an international breeding programme, and the two cubs born then are now in zoos in Frankfurt and Nürnberg.